FREEZE FRAME

AUTHOR BIO

B. David Warner

Dave Warner brings an intimate knowledge of the advertising industry to Freeze Frame. He has been in the driver's seat of advertising for products from cars to candy bars, and is thus no stranger to the world of fiction.

Having worked in the past for Ross Roy, Burton Sohigian, Campbell Ewald and Sarris & Associates, Warner is now Creative Director of a medium-sized Detroit-area advertising agency. He is at home in virtually every medium from novels and television to radio, print, outdoor and direct mail.

He is even more at home in Clarkston, Michigan, where he lives with his wife, Marlene, and their daughters Andi and Margi.

Warner is a graduate of Michigan State University, where he majored in advertising and journalism. He decided on advertising as a career because, he says, "I was too nervous to steal."

FREEZE FRAME

Tony —
Enjoy!
B David Warner
Great seeing you again!
Bob

By

B. David Warner

Pine Tar Books
(A branch of MidMerica Publishing Co.)
Stories that stick with you.

Pine Tar Books * CLARKSTON, MI * A branch of MidMerica Publishing Co.

Copyright © 2006

All rights reserved. Printed in the United States of America. No part of this publication may be reproduced, stored in a retrieval system, or transmitted, in any form or by any means electronic, mechanical, photocopying, recording, or otherwise, without the prior written permission of the author.

Although inspired by true events, in no way are any of the fictional characters and fictional situations intended to depict actual people or places.

ISBN 1-58961-502-6

Acknowledgements

The great author Arthur Hailey once began his acknowledgements by saying, "When you see a turtle up on a fencepost, you know someone had to put him there."

In Mr. Hailey's case, I think he was far too modest. But I share his sense of appreciation for the people who help and encourage a writer during the course of completing a novel, in this case, my first.

To Lt. Joseph Quisenberry of the Oakland County Sheriff's Department and Jim Saffold, former Detroit police officer, I extend my thanks for their help in explaining police policies and procedures. Any errors in this area are mine, certainly not theirs.

For suggestions in content and pacing, thanks go to Tom Barbas and William Hoffman. For invaluable help in setting up the manuscript thanks to Ron Bauer. For her efforts on behalf of Freeze Frame, I thank Myra Manning. For a phone call that caused me to pull the manuscript out of the drawer and give it a second chance, I'm indebted to Larry Askins and Ralph Keifer. For helpful suggestions and encouragement, thanks go to Alinda Rininger.

And for her patience and help, I thank Marlene, my wife. I dedicate this novel to her and to my daughters, Andi and Margi.

FACT:

As the result of rumors concerning American POWs being brainwashed by Chinese communists during the Korean War, CIA Director Allen Dulles authorized a top-secret program known as MKULTRA in April of 1953. The program financed ultra-sensitive medical and psychological experiments in mind control; the scope of which included areas such as truth drugs, hypnosis, sleep deprivation and subliminal persuasion. The more troubling aspects of MKULTRA became the subject of executive and congressional investigations during the 1970s.

While the government reported that MKULTRA was discontinued in 1966, much of the program's research remains highly classified.

1

No time to think, just react.

Mashing the accelerator to the floor, the power of the engine thrust me back into the seat as the Avatar AVX sprang forward, reeling in taillights from the darkness of the road straight ahead. In seconds a vehicle a hundred yards away was suddenly just a car length in front, its red taillights slipping to the right and disappearing as I whipped the Avatar around and past.

"Darcy!" In the passenger seat beside me, Sean Higgins stomped the floor in a vain attempt to slam on an imaginary brake. I wondered whether his anxiety sprang from the blinding speed of the seven hundred horsepower sports car or the fact that a female controlled the wheel.

A bright yellow Ford had pulled onto the road just ahead, oblivious to my Avatar eating up the street behind it. I slammed the brake pedal, pushed the clutch to the floor, downshifted and swerved left, flying past a shell-shocked driver.

Numbers on the digital speedometer blurred: sixty-four . . . eighty-five . . . fifty-three . . . forty–seven . . . fifty-eight.

My heart beat wildly; my mouth felt dry as dust.

In the mirror I saw the Dodge Viper in pursuit reflecting my moves; a pair of headlights dodging left to right, right to left across all three lanes.

From the moment I sat at the wheel of the Avatar AVX, this car felt special—the way the interior wrapped around me in the driver's seat and its acceleration pressed my body back into leather. I wished I could enjoy the experience now, but this ride threatened to turn deadly any second.

In spite of the Avatar's overwhelming power, the Viper gained rapidly. In heavy traffic I couldn't maintain a speed above sixty miles per hour for long. Slashing through slower vehicles, I alarmed drivers as I screamed past, causing them to pull aside, making it easy for the two men in the Viper to follow.

"Darcy!"

A giant semi dead ahead. I spun the wheel, nearly sideswiping a Jeep on the left, then pulled a hard right avoiding a pickup truck. I raced past and braked hard, downshifting, and barely missed becoming part of the backseat of a red Camaro. Swerving left, I found myself behind a Dodge Durango. I felt sure I had put pavement between the Viper and me, but no such luck. With the advantage of following in my tracks it now loomed just a car length behind.

Suddenly the Durango ahead turned right and I saw clear road.

Downshifting, I pounded the accelerator, our bodies slamming leather as the V-12 roared and speedometer digits blurred. Nothing could match this acceleration. Looking back,

I saw the Viper now trapped behind a gaggle of cars. The yellow eyes in the rearview mirror grew small.

An exhilarating three minutes passed before Metropolitan Parkway appeared dead ahead, the intersection empty but traffic signals burning bright red. With the Viper now gone from the rear view mirror, I killed the Avatar's lights and put it into a four-wheel drift, screaming into an illegal left turn. Tires shrieking against pavement, the car suddenly headed west, leaving Gratiot Avenue behind.

Thirty seconds passed before I switched the lights on and slowed to avoid attracting attention.

As the Avatar resumed normal speed, I glanced sideways at Higgins. The agency vice president who had pissed me off a few hours earlier by referring to the Avatar AVX as "a real man's car," now appeared shell shocked. His eyes were deer-in-the-headlights wide and as we passed under a streetlight I could see that all color had drained from his face. His lips were moving, trying to form words, but without sound. I spoke first.

"You're right. This is a real man's car."

2

What now?

How many were there? And how long before they came after us again, now that we held the DVD they'd proved so willing to kill for?

My body was coming down from a serious adrenalin high. I hadn't driven that fast in months, never on city streets. My heart still pounded, albeit slower, and I became aware of my palms—wet and slippery against the leather steering wheel.

A digital gauge on the instrument panel began blinking the news—the Avatar's fuel tank needed nourishment. Higgins slowly regained his composure as we turned into a Shell station off Metropolitan Parkway. He used a credit card at the pump farthest from the cashier's booth, filling the Avatar with high octane.

I thanked God I had kept up the training the Adams & Benson advertising agency provided its creative people five years ago. Back then it was common practice to send writers and art directors assigned to its American Vehicle Corporation account to the famous Skip Barber Racing School. They wanted us to have an intimate feel for the subjects of the ads we were assigned to create.

I took the training more seriously than my contemporaries. When I left Detroit after my divorce five years ago, I became a regular at the two-mile, fourteen-turn Grattan Track near Grand Rapids. There I practiced skills like heel-and-toe downshifting, trail breaking and finding the fastest racing lanes.

When AVC made plans to introduce this souped-up AVX version of their hot Avatar sports car last summer, company officials asked me, Darcy James, to drive one of the first prototypes. They wanted, get this, "a woman's opinion."

My opinion? The same as a man's—with a top speed well over two hundred miles an hour and a zero-to-sixty time under three seconds, this car was one fast mother.

I stayed in the driver's seat as we pulled back onto the road, checking the rearview mirror for signs of the Viper or the police. We drove aimlessly, both of us near shock from the events that had just taken place: the shooting of a policeman and the high-speed escape from two armed men. The image of the officer crumbling to the pavement kept tumbling through my mind. Had he died? Did he have a wife? Children? A feeling of sadness stuck to the mental picture.

To my right Higgins fumbled with the stereo; "I could use some 'Music to Relieve Stress By.'"

He found a newscast instead. We listened in horror as the breaking story unfolded; a police officer killed near Roseville, a community north of Detroit. Two males were being held for questioning; two other persons, a man and woman, had fled in a black Avatar. It would be a matter of hours, at most, before those "two other persons" were identified as Darcy James and

Sean Higgins, executives employed by the Adams & Benson advertising agency.

Higgins hit the "off" switch. "They're saying we killed that cop."

"Maybe we should get to the police and tell them what really happened."

"No. You can bet the two guys chasing us have already spilled their version. What chance do we have when the cops, including your former husband, already have me in their sights for another murder?"

I hated to admit Higgins was right. "It's our word against Bacalla and Roland's," I said. I glanced over at the small metallic disc in his hands. "We've got to find out why they're so desperate to get their hands on that DVD."

Higgins thought for a moment. "It keeps coming back to this disc and Vince Caponi."

"Yep."

I felt the impact of the situation wash over me. There seemed to be no one to turn to, and my fate was partially dependent on a man I couldn't stand to be in the same room with just days before.

With the police looking for us, driving the black Avatar was like riding around under a spotlight. I left the main road and meandered through side streets.

We rode in silence. At one point, as Higgins pulled out his cell phone and started punching a number, I stopped him.

"I've got to tell Cunningham we won't be at the presentation tomorrow morning," he said.

"Not on your cell. I read that police can pinpoint their location, like tracing any call. You can bet Bacalla's told them who we are. Let's find a pay phone."

Higgins agreed, but for the next few hours we simply drove, as if moving made us less vulnerable. Staying clear of major highways we wandered from side street to side street, from suburb to suburb, from late night to early morning.

Somehow we had to uncover what Vince Caponi found on that disc, but without suffering the same fate.

3

Ten Days Earlier
Friday, Oct 08—6:13 p.m.

A devout Roman Catholic, Vince Caponi would spend the last few moments of his life viewing a pornographic movie.

He would have had a logical explanation if Father Brezinski of St. Germaine's Parish had walked through the door instead of the killer.

The evening had begun with the prospect of another late session at United Color Studios. For the tenth day in a row Caponi found himself alone at the studio, camped in a dark, windowless editing suite surrounded by three naked white walls and a fourth covered by a dozen TV monitors. A control panel housing rows of dials and switches that operated those monitors ran the length of the wall.

Freeze Frame

To relieve the boredom, Caponi decided to rent a movie from the Video Giant that recently opened down the street. The plan called for running the movie on one monitor, while editing the commercial for American Vehicle Corporation on two of the other screens. The agency needed the finished spot the next morning, but after eight years in the business Caponi could turn out a thirty-second spot in his sleep.

Unfortunately, Video Giant's selection fell far short of its name. He had already seen the few current titles, and found nothing of interest in the older, classic video section. About to leave, he noticed a room marked "Adults Only." Entering, he discovered racks filled with DVD covers featuring pictures of the actors and actresses who cavorted on the provocative digital discs inside. One in particular caught his eye: *Titillating Ta-tas*. The attractive blonde on the cover looked oddly familiar. In fact, she could have been the identical twin of an actress in a certain AVC commercial he had edited a few months back. It couldn't possibly be the same woman . . . could it? He decided to check it out.

Back at United Color, he put *Titillating Ta-tas* up on Monitor A, fast-forwarding through the credits and freezing the frame as the blonde on the cover appeared wearing a seductive smile and little else. Next, he retrieved the single copy of the AVC commercial in question from the storage room. He inserted the disc labeled "Avion on the Beach" and hit the switch for Monitor B.

The commercial began with the Avion, AVC's top selling vehicle, parked on a beach and surrounded by a host of bikini-clad women. As the camera zoomed in for a close up, Caponi leaned forward in his chair. The blonde next to the car appeared to be a dead ringer for the woman smiling down at him from Monitor A. But whether she was more than just a look-alike he couldn't be certain. Turning a dial in front of him, he slowed the action on Monitor B until the commercial ran virtually frame-by-frame.

That's when he noticed something funny. *Strange funny.*

He felt unsure of what he saw, but it concerned him enough to call Darren Cato, the TV producer at Adams & Benson, the advertising agency that filmed the spot. Finding Cato long gone on a Friday evening, he left a voicemail message. Then he burned two copies of the commercial, put the discs into clear plastic protective covers and inserted each in a cardboard envelope. He enclosed a short note in Cato's package, called to arrange a special pickup, and carried both outside to the FedEx box at the front door.

A ringing nightline greeted him back in the editing suite. The caller turned out to be someone at the agency who had heard his message for Cato; a name he didn't recognize. The man told him not to worry about his discovery; the disc must have been sent to United Color by mistake. Said he'd send someone to pick it up. Caponi hung up and unlocked the studio's back door.

Returning to the editing suite, he began thinking about what he had seen. He hit the button on the Sony machine and replayed the commercial. When he got to the blonde, he slowed the action once again. That's when the significance of the aberration dawned on him. He sat stunned; realizing the brief note he had enclosed in the package to Cato wasn't enough. *No, my god, not nearly enough.*

He ran out to the FedEx box, finding the two copies gone. *Damn. FedEx must have had a truck in the neighborhood when he called.*

Caponi dashed back in, careful to lock the front door. As he returned to the suite he heard a noise from the rear of the building—the messenger coming for the disc. He couldn't let him have it, not now.

He had to tell someone what he had found. Caponi reached for the telephone and dialed Cato's home number. He got the usual "your call is important" message after the fourth ring and began to speak into the receiver, leaving a detailed message.

He felt rather than saw the figure in the open doorway and began to turn when the nine millimeter hollow point ripped through his cheek, shattering teeth and taking out part of the roof of his mouth before tearing through the other side.

That bullet would have made certain he never talked again, but it wasn't enough for the man now four feet from the back of Caponi's head. A second hollow point ripped through his brain, blowing his forehead open and painting the control board with blood, cerebrospinal fluid and bits of bone and brain tissue.

What remained of Caponi's head crashed against the control board amidst a spreading pool of red just below the blonde on Monitor B, still smiling, oblivious to the blob of crimson matter now oozing down the screen.

4

Now

We had driven for hours in the darkness when we spotted a Meijer discount department store on M-59.

The sign outside trumpeted 24-hour service, but the only vehicles in the brightly lit parking lot were the half dozen employees' cars parked in a cluster seventy feet from the entrance. I noticed a vacant spot near the center of the formation and eased the Avatar in. Higgins and I got out and headed for the store.

I hoped the Avatar would go unnoticed, but glancing over my shoulder, it looked like a lion among a group of pussycats.

Good thing the store was deserted. Noticing our reflections in the store window on the way in, I realized we'd be hard to miss, even in a crowd. Higgins, dressed carefully in black to match—*oh brother!*—the Avatar he drove earlier in the day, stood a rangy six-three. His pretty boy Brad Pitt look was saved by a nose. That is, a proboscis that looked like it might have been bashed a time or two in "The Big House" where he played football for the University of Michigan.

I had grown up sensitive about my height, somewhere just under six feet in heels, thinking of myself as the typical gawky teenager. A more comfortable feeling of "self" came later when I played point guard for the Michigan State basketball team that went to the Final Four my junior year, and got voted onto the Homecoming Court as a senior. Now the reflection in the window showed a woman in her early thirties, with light brown hair that fell just below her shoulders, dressed in the navy pantsuit her father had given her. Dad and I had grown especially close since Mom died six years ago, and I treasured the outfit.

All in all, I thought, the picture wasn't bad for a once ugly duckling.

We found a bank of telephones inside the sliding glass doors. Higgins pushed coins into the first and entered Ken Cunningham's home number. He cocked the receiver so I could hear. The Adams & Benson executive vice president picked up after the fifth ring.

"Hello."

"Ken? Sean Higgins."

"What time is it?"

"Quarter to five, Ken. I've got to talk to you."

"What is it?" Cunningham suddenly snapped wide-awake.

"You're going to have to give the presentation to AVC management alone this morning, Ken."

"What?"

Higgins went through the story, starting with the Avion disc, the car chase and ultimately, the shooting of the policeman.

"Where's the DVD now?" Cunningham asked.

"We've got it."

"Are you sure it's the disc they're after?"

"Ken, three people are dead, another is lying in a coma. That DVD figured in at least three cases and probably all four."

"Who wants it and why?"

"I wish I knew."

"You said the disc contained an Avion commercial . . . the one with all those bikini-clad women on the beach."

"That's right."

"Hell, we ran that thing six months ago. Don't see why anyone would want it now. But bring the DVD to me," Cunningham said, "I'll have it checked out."

"Too risky, Ken. We've got to get out of town."

"Where are you going?"

"My uncle's cottage near Gaylord."

"Not a good idea. The police'll look for you there."

"Not unless someone tips them off. The uncle is my mother's brother. His last name's different from mine."

"I still think you'll be safer somewhere else. Let me do some checking. Where can I call you?"

"I'm at a pay phone. I'll have to call you."

"Give me fifteen minutes."

Now it was my turn to make a call. I started to dial.

"Who are you calling?" Higgins asked.

"Garry Kaminski. I want someone on the police force to hear our side of the story."

"Okay, but make it quick. I'll be inside grabbing a cup of coffee."

The phone rang six times before my former husband answered.

"Kaminski. You'd better have a damn good reason calling this early."

"Garry . . . it's Darcy."

"Darcy? Where the hell are you? The Roseville police put out an APB on you and your buddy Higgins. Our desk sergeant recognized your name and called me after midnight."

"Garry, I swear the shooting wasn't our fault. Another man held the gun. Higgins reached for it, and it went off."

"Darcy, the two guys they arrested in the Viper are telling their version of the story. Every badge in town is looking for you. You've got to come in."

"Garry, you don't understand . . ."

"I understand they've got a description of you and Higgins in a black Avatar, and you're lucky you haven't been picked up already."

"But there were witnesses."

"Three witnesses say Higgins shot the cop, three say the other guy shot him, one says it looked like an accident. But the two other guys are talking and you're not."

"It's that disc Vince Caponi had, Garry. It's at the bottom of everything."

"Darcy, you're betting your *life* on that. Think about it. Higgins is the prime suspect in one murder and now he's wanted for another.

"Look, my caller ID's got the number you're calling from. Stay there, I'll come get you."

With the Roseville police looking for us, and a Detroit cop who also happened to be my ex-husband racing our way, I had to do something.

5

Twenty minutes later, Higgins sat sipping from a Styrofoam cup as I approached him from behind.

"Let's get on the road."

Startled, Higgins choked on his coffee. He looked up. "I need to get back to Cunningham."

"Call him later. Kaminski's on the way. We've got to get out of here. Now."

We started walking quickly—out of the small coffee shop, past the sleepy cashier manning the only open register, through the automatic doors and into the parking lot.

The cars hunched in the small group were still the only vehicles in the lot. As we approached them, I wondered how long it would take Higgins to notice.

"Where's the Avatar?"

"Over there," I pointed. "The white one."

"The *white* one? What the hell do you mean, the *white one?*"

"I painted it."

"You . . . *what*?" We were now standing next to a very low, very white, Avatar AVX.

"It took five cans of touch-up paint. They were on sale. Didn't you see the display?"

"Are *you* nuts?" Higgins' face was beet red. "You've screwed up a sixty-thousand-dollar paint job. It took six weeks to get it right. By hand."

"Are you nuts? The cops are looking for a *black* Avatar. They find it, we're in prison. For *life*." Higgins had to admit I was right. While the AVX was a prototype with a much more powerful engine than the standard Avatar, it shared the body style familiar to sports car enthusiasts around the country. The white color would give us a better chance at freedom.

I held his gaze. "Now, are you driving, or am I?"

Higgins held the keys. A touch of the remote button and the car's gullwing doors unfolded.

"Watch the paint," I said, sliding into the passenger seat. "It's wet." Higgins shot me a sour look. A turn of the key provoked a snarl from the engine.

Pulling out of the parking lot onto M-59, Higgins kept to the right, melding into the morning rush hour. Watching oncoming traffic, I saw my former husband, the cop, speed by in the opposite direction.

I couldn't help smiling as I thought of him running around the store looking for us.

"I heard you tell Ken Cunningham you have relatives up north," I said.

"My aunt and uncle have a cottage in Gaylord, about forty miles below the Mackinac Bridge."

"Think they'll put up a couple of fugitives?"

"They're in Florida."

"We're going to break in?"

"I know where they hide the key."
But would we make it that far?

6

Seven Days Earlier
Monday, Oct. 11–9:15 a.m.

I hadn't known Vince Caponi, but news of his death touched me. Years ago, married to a Detroit street cop, violence became my constant companion. When I divorced Garry Kaminski, I thought I had jilted that companion too, leaving it behind when I bolted for Grand Rapids. Now, returning to the Motor City, I found my old nemesis on hand to greet me the first day on the job.

When Garry and I split, too much of my former husband remained in the places we had known— the Fox Theatre District, Greek Town, Belle Isle— for me to feel comfortable anywhere near them.

I moved back to Grand Rapids. My father, alone after Mom's death, welcomed me home, and at first the situation seemed comfortable as the proverbial old shoe. But I soon realized my hometown had become several sizes too small.

Nearly five years passed before the call came from Ken Cunningham, Adams & Benson's executive vice president and an old family friend. The position of creative supervisor on the American Vehicle Corporation account had opened. I'd been recommended by A & B's executive creative director, my former boss, Sid Goldman. "And by the way," Ken had added, "Sid had a heart attack. He almost died."

After getting past the shock of Sid's heart attack, I weighed the proposition. The job paid well and I'd be back writing about my first love: cars. The truth is, I know more about wheels than most men.

Two weeks later I moved back to Detroit.

My office turned out to be on six, a floor routinely sealed off from the rest of the agency during the months of creative planning for next year's AVC models. You needed a key to open the door when the elevator stopped there. I learned that because of this tight security, the account team of Niles VanBuhler, third party candidate for President of the United States, had insisted on taking over half of the floor when they moved here from D.C. three months ago.

As I stood gazing out the floor-to-ceiling window of my new office, the view of the Detroit River with Windsor, Ontario, on the other side was breathtaking. I could see a cabin cruiser bouncing eastward, fighting white-capped waves toward Lake St. Clair. To my right, the cylindrical towers of the Renaissance Center shot into the sky. Below, the A & B parking lot stretched two hundred feet along the river.

I vowed to do something about the bare wall on my left soon. I'd been an avid art collector since college, scraping together dollars to buy a lithograph by one artist or another. My favorite genre was the American Southwest and painters like Remington, Russell, Inness and Whittredge. My collection remained in Grand Rapids. I'd bring a few lithographs next trip, to cover some of that wall space.

A stack of folders sat on the center of my desk, each containing a work profile of the writers and art directors on my new staff. I had known a couple from my previous stint at A & B, but several had joined the agency in the interim. I spent the morning reviewing the profiles.

I'd be lying if I said I hadn't been nervous about taking this job: a huge step from a small town to directing the creative product of an account spending nearly a billion dollars in a single year. Every creative person goes through periods of self-doubt, and right now I had to fight to keep those thoughts at bay.

"Just because it's your first day doesn't mean you can't break for lunch."

Startled, I looked up from the last profile to see a six-foot-two male of African American descent in the doorway. I recognized Matt Carter from the photograph in his personnel file. Behind him stood two others: a short, dark-complected man in a blue striped short-sleeved shirt and a taller, sandy-haired man in a business suit.

"Hi, Darcy, I'm Matt Carter and your two other lunch companions are Manny Rodriguez and Paul Chapman."

The shorter man, Manny Rodriguez, smiled and nodded. "Nice meeting you, Darcy. I like the work you did on the Avatar last time you were here. Your ads remind me of the early Volkswagen campaign." I had just finished reading Rodriguez' folder. A late bloomer, he had joined Adams & Benson as a copywriter after a long career in the Army.

"We promise we won't let Manny bore you," said the taller man, Chapman. "He's a walking encyclopedia of advertising trivia."

"You account guys are all alike," Rodriguez smiled. "You don't care about the creative product as long as you have directions to the client's country club."

"Somebody's got to schmooze the clients so they'll approve the copy you write," Chapman said.

Carter turned to me. "Paul's a scratch golfer, except when he's playing a client."

"I had to hit eight balls into the water last Thursday, to keep from kicking Denny Desnoyer's butt by more than fifteen strokes," Chapman said.

"I'm surprised Desnoyer did that well," said Carter. "How he swings a club past that gut of his ranks with the mysteries of the pyramids and the missing link."

"Speaking of stomachs," Rodriguez said, "mine's empty as a vp's office on Friday afternoon. Let's go."

"You're sure I won't be in the way of some kind of male bonding session?" I asked.

"You kidding?" Rodriguez said. "How can you bond with guys who don't even know what a gerund is?"

The repartee continued as we left the building heading for Big Norm's Restaurant two blocks away.

At one point I heard Carter whisper to Chapman, "What the hell is a gerund anyway?"

"I'm not sure," Chapman whispered back. "I think it's one of those old golf clubs. Like a mashie or a spoon."

"Be worth a lot of money, you had one in good condition."

"Damn straight."

7

To paraphrase Yogi Berra, lunch at Big Norm's Restaurant turned out to be "déjà vu all over again."

I'd been inside Big Norm's last during my bon voyage affair five years ago, and as we approached the well-manicured old building memories danced in my head.

The sign in front advertised "A Dining Experience," but to Adams & Benson employees who treated its elegant lounge like a neighborhood bar every night after five, it would more accurately have read: "A Drinking Experience."

Now *that* would have been truth in advertising.

As we walked through the front door, Willis, Big Norm's tall, distinguished maitre d', greeted me with a hug. We asked to be seated in the lounge and got the last table, a white-cloth-covered four-top just inside the door. It was SRO at the bar itself, and waiters and waitresses hustled drinks from the service bar to tables, and carried trays filled with the seafood dishes that put Big Norm's on the culinary map. As we sat down,

I couldn't help notice that a tall, wiry, red-haired man in the crowd at the bar seemed to be staring our way.

"Matt, did you know the guy who was killed last night?" Manny Rodriguez asked as he unfolded a white cloth napkin.

"Caponi? Yeah. Darren Cato and I used his studio a lot. Vince and I golfed once or twice, and I had dinner with him and his wife a few times. I can't believe he's gone."

"Murdered," Chapman said with an exaggerated shiver. "Who would kill a guy like that?"

"Do the police have a motive?" I asked. Glancing toward the bar, I noticed the red-haired man continued to glare toward our table. His attention seemed focused on me, but why? It was my first day here after five years.

"The motive wasn't robbery," Carter said. "Vince had a wallet full of money and credit cards."

A waiter appeared, setting menus and a basket of Big Norm's hot-from-the-oven onion rolls on the table. He retrieved a notebook from his pocket and took drink orders. The redhead at the bar continued to stare my way.

"Have you had the dubious pleasure of meeting Sean Higgins?" Chapman asked as the waiter left. He apparently had heard enough talk about violence.

"What do you mean, *dubious pleasure*?" I asked, my attention returning to the table. I knew Higgins by name only. He had joined Adams & Benson as account head of the American Vehicle Corporation business during the five years I had been gone. I knew we'd be working together, and my title as creative supervisor meant, in theory, we were equals.

"I mean you won't find many creative people worshipping at the shrine of Sean Higgins," Chapman said.

"Let me put it in less religious terms," Carter smiled. "Sean Higgins thinks creative people are more interested in doing commercials that win awards, than in selling the client's product."

"That's ridiculous," I said. "We're merely trying to create print and broadcast advertising that stands out . . . that breaks through the clutter."

"Tell that to Higgins," Carter said. "If you get the chance. When it comes to dealing with creative people, he has the tact of a pit bull on steroids."

"Darren Cato found that out," said Rodriguez. "Remember the time he walked into Higgins' office with his shades on?"

"Yeah," said Chapman. "It wasn't so much the sunglasses as Cato's way of strutting around in them. He's a producer-type, thinks he's strictly Hollywood. Higgins brought the meeting to a screeching halt and made Cato leave his sunglasses out in the hallway."

"That's Sean Higgins," laughed Carter, "pure hard ass. He thinks he's still playing football for the University of Michigan."

Rodriguez turned to me. "You'll have to excuse Matt, he's never gotten over the fact that Higgins didn't fall for his memo."

I had to ask. "What memo?"

Rodriguez leaned forward, his smile widening. "Rumor has it that Matt, here, was responsible for a certain memo sent to all employees under the signature of one of the senior vps. The memo requested that account executives drink whiskey instead of vodka at lunch."

"Whiskey? Why?"

"So that during afternoon meetings clients would know the account executives were drunk, not just stupid."

That got the table laughing. In the middle of it, the waiter appeared to distribute the drinks. He pulled the pad from his pocket and waited for our food order.

"I haven't even had time to look," I said, reaching for the menu.

"Big Norm's is famous for broiled salmon," Chapman said.

"Salmon it is."

One by one, the others ordered and the waiter left, snaking through the crowd at the bar where people now stood two deep.

"Hey, look . . . Baron Nichols." Carter pointed to the red-haired man who had been staring at me from the bar. Catching Nichols' eye, he waved him to our table.

"Baron, meet Darcy James," Carter said as Nichols approached. "She's the new group creative head on AVC."

I held out a hand that Nichols ignored, instead staring coolly into my eyes. "I hope she can handle it," he said. Then the arrogant bastard left to rejoin his group.

"You could scrape the ice off that greeting," Rodriguez said. "I heard Nichols had a screaming match with Ken Cunningham when you got the job as AVC creative head instead of him, but there's no excuse for that behavior."

"No harm done," I said. "Believe me, I've encountered worse."

Truthfully, I felt more angered than embarrassed by Nichols' snub. And while he may have acted like an ass, there seemed no point making an issue of it.

8

Chapman finally broke the embarrassed silence that followed, changing the subject. "I hear Darren Cato didn't show up for his meeting with the VanBuhler people."

"Yeah, said Carter, "his girlfriend's Sue Askins; the woman in Research? She tried to call him all morning. She left just before lunch to check his house."

"He'd better not miss many meetings with those people," Rodriguez said. "Have you seen that guy Bacalla? He looks like he sprinkles guys like Cato on his breakfast cereal."

"What's happening on the VanBuhler campaign anyway, Paul?" Carter asked. "We haven't seen much of you since you got assigned to the team. You must be important."

"Yeah, tell me about it. Fact is I'm more go-fer than executive. Bob Bacalla quarterbacks all the plays."

Rodriguez reached for another roll. "Is he as mean as he looks?"

"He's tough to read," said Chapman. "I've worked with him for weeks and I know less about him than when I started."

I jumped in. "The election's coming up fast, Paul. How about a prediction?"

"It's going to be a lot tighter than people expect."

I had been following the campaigning. "For a third-party candidate, VanBuhler sure ate up the primaries. New Hampshire, Massachusetts, Illinois . . ."

Entering the race as an independent, Niles VanBuhler straddled the fence on virtually every issue. His boyish, suntanned good looks and impeccably combed, prematurely silver hair played well with the press. When it came to sound bites, the guy was a piranha. With the election just weeks away, VanBuhler's popularity rivaled that of the incumbent, David Nordstrum.

"What does VanBuhler's contingent say about his mysterious success?" Carter asked.

"Nothing, nada, zero," Chapman said. "Funny thing is, they don't seem all that surprised."

The waiter interrupted, setting steaming dishes in front of each person. My plate held a salmon steak nearly three-quarters of an inch thick.

A sudden ringing came from somewhere close. Carter set his fork on the plate and reached for his pager.

"Ain't technology great?" he said. "Even without my cell phone, the office can find me anywhere." He stood up and headed for the sole pay telephone near the restrooms.

"Poor Matt," said Rodriguez. "It's not enough to be a producer, he's trying to be a writer, too. The guy's been running his butt off."

Chapman started to speak, but stopped as he noticed Carter hurrying back.

"A package just arrived," Carter said, taking a quick bite of whitefish without sitting down. "It's addressed to Darren Cato. Since he's AWOL they plopped it on my desk."

"What's the hurry?" Chapman asked.

Carter took a gulp from his water glass and set it back on the table.

"The package is from Vince Caponi."

9

Now

Riding north on a concrete ribbon, we twisted past the factories of Flint, the factory outlets of Birch Run, up and over the mammoth Zilwaukee Bridge, winding around Saginaw and Bay City, then straight through mile after mile of flat brown autumn fields that reached out to touch the horizon.

Just when it seemed the land in this part of the state grew nothing but monotony, trees closed in on either side of the highway and we were in Michigan's north country. I peered out the side window and took in a blur of autumn reds, oranges and yellows, interrupted by the occasional dark green of a stand of pine.

I had forgotten how hilly northern Michigan could be. One moment I stared up fifty-foot embankments on either side; the next, I gazed down as the shoulder dropped into a valley thirty feet below. I was admiring the landscape when Higgins turned to me.

"Guess I owe you an apology."

"Oh?" *An apology? From Sean Higgins?* I smiled, recalling Matt Carter's comment: "an apology from Higgins comes about as often as a neutered Cocker Spaniel."

"You knew Bacalla and Roland were up to something," he said. "Personally, I think it's industrial espionage."

"They're evil, alright. But their game's not industrial espionage."

"It isn't? But you . . ."

"Thought at first they were spying on our ad campaign for the new Ampere. I know."

"And now . . ."

"You're not going to say my imagination's running wild?"

"After what's happened anything is possible. My mind is as open as one of those giant beach umbrellas."

"Alright. You've heard of subliminal persuasion?"

"You mean that BS about the sub-conscious picking up messages invisible to the eye?"

"BS, huh? Where's that giant beach umbrella?"

"My mind is always open. But that doesn't mean it accepts every hare-brained thought that comes along."

"I admit it's a stretch, but something Manny Rodriguez said the night he called sticks in my mind. He mentioned the words subliminal persuasion."

"He said he found a subliminal message on that disc?"

"Not exactly. He told me to come over right away, which I did, finding him nearly beaten to death."

"So you don't know for a fact he found a subliminal message on the disc."

"No." We rode in silence for a while.

"Assuming you're right," Sean said finally, "and I don't believe for a moment you are, what kind of subliminal message would be on that disc?"

"Whatever's on it, Bacalla and Roland are desperate to get it back." I said. "I think somehow it involves drugs or drug cartels."

I wanted to describe my conversation with Sid Goldman yesterday afternoon; a meeting that now seemed an eternity ago. I recalled my former creative director's suspicions concerning Bacalla and his telephone calls to Tijuana.

Remembering Sid's shaking hands and the threats to his granddaughter's life, I kept the conversation to myself.

Higgins stared at the road ahead. "If you're right, we're in ahell of a lot more trouble than we thought."

10

Monday, Oct. 11–1:13 p.m.

The FedEx package listed Darren Cato as the addressee, but Carter didn't hesitate to tear it open.

Inside he found a square, flat plastic carton; the type designed to hold DVDs or CD-ROMs. The label on the disc inside was clearly visible: *Avion On the Beach :30 Submaster copy*. Chapman, Rodriguez and I watched as Carter popped the container open and removed the disc. A piece of paper packed with it fell to the floor. Carter picked it up.

"It's from Caponi," he said, glancing at the paper and then back to the three of us. "It says, *Hey Cato, what the hell's with this DVD?*"

"Maybe it's blank," Chapman said.

"Doesn't figure he'd make a big deal over a blank disc," Rodriguez said.

Carter nodded. "Let's run it on the big screen up on seven and see."

A half-dozen run-throughs in the screening room turned up nothing unusual. The disc contained a commercial exactly as I remembered seeing it on TV: an Avion automobile screaming over Daytona Beach sand, its movements choreographed to a strong jazz beat. As the car halts, it's surrounded by a group of bikini-clad women. The ad stood as proof that beer commercials don't have a corner on mindless male chauvinism.

As the lights came up I found the men looking my way, waiting for a reaction.

"We won't be doing commercials like that while I'm in charge of creative," I said.

"The whole thing was Murphy's idea." Rodriguez sounded defensive. "He's AVC's vice president of advertising. The guy loves to go off on location with a bunch of good-looking babes."

"It was embarrassing," Carter said. "They scrapped the thing after two or three weeks."

The phone rang. I was closest. "Screening room, James."

"Ms. James, is Matt Carter with you?" asked the voice.

"He is."

"There's a policeman in the lobby to see him."

"There's a cop downstairs for you," I said to Carter.

Carter took the receiver. "Put him on, Mary." Matt listened for a moment. "That's right. I worked with Vince. On a number of projects. And I worked with Cato."

Silence again. "You're welcome to come up to my office and ask questions. But you might be interested in a DVD Caponi sent to the agency the night he died. We're screening it now."

Carter set the phone in the cradle. "He's coming up."

A few minutes later, the shock that went through me couldn't have been worse if I'd touched a live wire.

"Garry!" It felt like someone pushed a "reverse" button on my life and sent it reeling back five years. In the doorway to the screening room stood my ex-husband. He still carried his two hundred pounds well on a six-foot-one frame, but his hair was short. And that *suit*. When we married, Garry had been a narc; his uniform jeans and sweatshirts. He wore earrings and a ring through an eyebrow.

Known as the best actor on the force, Garry could talk his way into a crack house and make a buy; the inside man during a bust. But now the surprise on his face was real.

"Da . . . Darcy," he stammered. "I thought you were in Grand Rapids."

"I moved back this week. What are you doing here?"

"Investigating a murder . . . at least one. Guy named Vince Caponi. I understand he edited TV commercials for this company." Regaining his composure, he turned to the three men. "I'm Sergeant Kaminski. I got questions for Mr. Carter."

"I'm Matt Carter. What do you mean, *at least one murder?*"

"Sorry. I guess you haven't heard."

"Heard what?" I asked.

"Darren Cato. He worked here?"

"Yeah. What about him?" Carter asked.

"Sorry to break the news. His girl friend found him an hour ago. Hanged, in his living room."

"My god," I said. "Hanged? Suicide?"

"His girl friend says no, and she's plenty emphatic. They had plans for dinner tonight."

"So, what are you doing about it?" Chapman asked.

"We're investigating. That's all I can say." Garry turned to Matt Carter. "You said something about a DVD on the phone."

"An AVC commercial Caponi sent to Darren Cato. They worked on the commercial together months ago." He handed the note to my ex-husband. "Sounds like he found something on the DVD."

Garry scanned the piece of paper. "This Caponi's handwriting?"

"I've worked with him enough to recognize it."

"Well, what the hell *is* with that DVD?"

"Nothing," I said. "We've looked at it half a dozen times."

"Want to see it?" Carter asked.

"You bet I do." Standing hands on hips, Garry watched the large screen as Matt pressed the remote to rerun the commercial. When it finished, Garry spoke: "What's unusual about a bunch of women on a beach? Why would he bother sending it to you?"

The ringing of the telephone cut off any attempt at an answer. I reached for it: "James."

"Ms. James, I was hoping I'd find you," said the voice. "This is Tricia, Ken Cunningham's administrative assistant. Joe Adams and Mr. Cunningham are calling a meeting of all agency employees. Ken insisted I track you down."

"What's it about?"

"All I know, it's an emergency."

"Where and when?"

"Three o'clock, first floor lobby. Please pass the word to the others with you."

I looked at my watch. Two fifteen. The reason for the meeting wouldn't be a mystery long.

11

2:54 p.m.

Adams & Benson's cylindrical-shaped "Glass Palace" and adjacent parking lots cover five acres on the bank of the Detroit River, just east of the Renaissance Center.

The building's spectacular three-story lobby brings first-time visitors to their knees. Entering glass doors at the front of the building, their attention is immediately drawn to the thirty-foot waterfall at the far south end. The sound of water crashing into the pool at its base reverberates throughout the lobby.

On the second and third floor levels, glass-walled offices ring the lobby on three sides. A stairway just inside the front doors runs up ten feet to a round, carpeted mezzanine area, then twists and continues to the second floor. Twenty feet in diameter, the mezzanine creates an ideal speaking platform for an executive addressing a crowd below.

Minutes before three o'clock I stood just feet from that mezzanine, among a crowd of some five hundred A & B workers. Speculation buzzed about the reason for the meeting, but the consensus held it had something to do with the VanBuhler campaign. The crowd noise subsided as Ken Cunningham, Joe Adams and A & B board chairman C. J. Rathmore appeared at the head of the stairway on the second floor. They descended to the round mezzanine, Cunningham in the lead. Once they reached the platform, it surprised me to see that neither the chairman nor president stepped forward to speak. It was Ken Cunningham.

I hadn't seen Ken in years, but he hadn't changed. In a voice as rough as sandpaper, familiar as an old friend, he began to speak. He started with the announcement of Darren Cato's death. A collective gasp came from the crowd, but I couldn't help noticing the reactions were more shock than sorrow. Carter had been right: even a dead Darren Cato didn't rate much sympathy from his fellow workers.

After a pause to let the news settle, Cunningham went on. He spent a few moments directing accolades at agency employees, telling them what a great job they were all doing. Then he dropped the bomb.

"This morning the American Vehicle Corporation informed Joe Adams that after more than ninety years with Adams & Benson, they're going to conduct a review of advertising agencies."

Another gasp filled the lobby. A review meant AVC was considering other agencies, and losing the AVC account would mean a horrendous loss of jobs.

Suddenly landing a position at A & B didn't seem so fortunate after all. When an advertising agency loses a major account, the ax falls. The rule is usually "last in, first out." I rubbed the back of my neck.

Looking around, I saw a sea of tight, worried faces. People stood with arms crossed, brows furrowed. A few women dabbed at their eyes with tissues.

"The rules of the review are simple," Cunningham said. "AVC has a new model they're rushing onto the market. They've shared their marketing objectives with us, and with Simpson & Dancer and Chase Hilton, the agencies handling the other AVC divisions. The company creating what AVC considers the best campaign will be awarded all AVC advertising in the future. There will be two losers, and only one winner.

"Sean Higgins and his group will tackle this project immediately. I hope you'll all have a chance to meet our new creative supervisor, Darcy James, in the next few days." Cunningham smiled and nodded as he looked my way. "Her team of writers and art directors will spearhead the creative, working under tight security."

Cunningham paused and looked around before continuing. "That's it for now. You'll be kept up to date on developments as they occur. Sean Higgins and I will meet with Darcy James' creative group in the eighth floor conference room at four o'clock."

Cunningham did an abrupt about face and walked back up the stairs, followed by the other two men.

As stunned employees returned to their offices, the lobby emptied like a balloon losing its air.

12

News of the agency review seemed even more surprising given the history of the two companies. Adams & Benson and the American Vehicle Corporation were, as executives of both companies liked to say, "joined at the hip."

Bicker Adams, a one-time salesman for the Rembly Motor Car Company, founded the agency. His famous slogan, "No Car Rides Like a Rembly," carved awareness for the automobile, and accelerated it past dozens of choices the American public faced in the mid-twenties.

The agency blossomed in that decade, but like many companies nearly went out of business in the Thirties.

Expansion came in the Fifties. Adams Advertising purchased a smaller agency owned by James Benson. Benson Advertising brought a variety of accounts like Bassline Fishing Boats and Haraday Inns into the fold.

Changes took place at the Rembly Motor Car Company, too. Rembly merged with two other manufacturers in the post-war Forties to become the American Vehicle Corporation.

The following decades saw both companies prosper, and by the merger-happy Seventies, A & B's profitability attracted buyout offers from a number of larger firms. Bicker Adams insisted he would never sell, and he didn't. His son Joe did, years after his father's death. The buyer: Solomon & Solomon, a British holding company. The purchase agreement stipulated that Joe Adams remain at A & B as president. C. J. Rathmore, a Solomon & Solomon corporate vp from London, came to Detroit recently as A & B's chairman of the board.

The trade press blamed the sale on Adams & Benson's need for capital to replace the outlandish sum spent on their magnificent new building. But rumors persisted that Joe Adams himself had been responsible. His well-known penchant for gambling rivaled his love for liquor. According to the stories, he and his friend Niles VanBuhler had combined the two vices during a whirlwind trip to the Bahamas almost exactly a year ago. The result for Joe Adams had been an eight million dollar loss at the crap tables. When Solomon & Solomon appeared with an offer to buy the agency, their timing appeared perfect. They caught Adams in desperate need of cash and eager to consummate the deal.

The sale hadn't stopped Adams' gambling, especially now that Detroit had casinos of its own. But at least A & B staffers could stop worrying about their agency changing hands after every Adams binge.

13

3:21 p.m.

I returned to my office reeling from Cunningham's speech.

Dropping into the chair behind my desk, I noticed the light on my phone blinking. It turned out to be a voice mail message from Jeff Luden, a friend and Vice President at Luden Freeman Advertising in Chicago. I'd called him weeks ago when I became restless in Grand Rapids. I didn't feel like talking to anyone at the moment, but curiosity got the best of me.

He picked up the phone on the second ring. "Luden."

"Jeff, Darcy James."

"Hey, Darcy. Wish I could talk, but I've got a meeting in five minutes. We're in desperate need of a senior creative person here. Sorry to be abrupt, but I've got to cut to the chase. What would it take to hire you?"

Right now, not much. But could I really resign after just one day on the job?

"Look, Darcy, whatever you're making at A & B, I know we can go at least twenty K better. Let me know."

With that he was gone, leaving me staring at the receiver in my hand. It took a moment to recover and play a second voice mail message, simple and to the point: Ken Cunningham wanted to see me in his office immediately.

* * *

I found Ken behind an oak desk the size of Vermont. He stood and walked around the desk as I entered the room.

I stuck out my hand, which Ken ignored, grabbing me in a bear hug.

"Darcy. Good to have you back."

The embrace conjured up fond memories. Ken had been a close friend of the family and a frequent visitor to my parents' home. "How's your father?"

"Dad's fine. You know he remarried."

"Yes, sorry I missed the wedding. Bad timing. Is he still in Grand Rapids?"

"No. With me gone, he and Melanie—his new wife—didn't need that big house. They bought a condo just outside the city limits."

Ken stood back and looked me up and down in a fatherly sort of way. "You've certainly grown into a fine young lady, Darcy. It's hard to believe you're the same little girl your dad used to call 'Kitten.'"

"He still does." I laughed. "But at least he's shortened it to 'Kit.'"

"I know your dad's active as ever in politics. His name's on the guest list of every fund raiser the Dems throw. Wish he'd support our guy, VanBuhler, though."

"Afraid that's impossible, Ken. You know Dad . . . die-hard Democrat. It would be sacrilege to vote for a third party candidate."

Cunningham had been active in mainstream politics as a Republican. As early as high school, he and Dad had fallen on opposite sides of major issues, and both enjoyed the debates that ensued. As they grew older, Ken's resemblance to the old Democratic House Speaker Tip O'Neil became a constant source of ribbing from my dad.

Ken's face grew somber. "That announcement downstairs must have been a hell of a shock, Darcy. Especially coming on the heels of Darren Cato's death."

Ken waited for a reaction. I hadn't known Cato, and when I didn't show one, he went on.

"I want you to know that AVC's announcement came as a huge surprise to me as well." He motioned to one of the four plush leather chairs in front of his desk.

I had never seen Ken so serious. "Bill Kesler, AVC's Chairman, called Joe Adams this morning. Didn't have the guts to call me. Anyway, even my contacts at AVC were in the dark."

"And you found out . . ."

"When Adams broke the news at lunch. Just ten of us there. He wanted to keep the whole damn thing secret. We talked him out of that. But he didn't want to make the speech. I got elected."

I nodded. It reminded me of the old Cadillac ad: *The Penalty of Leadership*.

"As I said downstairs, Darcy, I have great confidence in you and your team."

I swallowed hard. "Thanks, Ken. You can count on us."

"One thing." Cunningham took a breath. "Baron Nichols' group will take a shot at it along with yours."

"Nichols? Ken, if you don't think . . ."

Cunningham held up a hand. "Believe me Darcy, it's not any lack of confidence in your team."

"Why, then?"

"Politics. Nichols demanded to be included. Any other time, I'd have told him to shove it. But right now, dissension is the last thing we need. The matter's settled, and I'll have more to tell all of you at four o'clock."

14

3:40 p.m.

I found my creative team waiting in my office. In the excitement of the announcement, I had nearly forgotten about the meeting I had scheduled earlier.

Three women and a young man who looked like a high school senior sat around my glass top table. Matt Riggs, Manny Rodriguez and a forty-ish man wearing a cowboy hat, boots and jeans occupied the chairs in front of my desk. From the personnel files, I guessed the man in cowboy garb as Bob Roy Pickard, a legendary copywriter from the Lone Star State.

"Sorry I'm late," I said. "This get-acquainted meeting's going to be short. Our four-o'clock get together with Cunningham and Higgins doesn't leave much time, so let's get started.

"First, my name is Darcy James." Glancing around the room, my eyes stopped at two of the women seated at the table: Ginny Stankowski, an extremely talented art director and M. J. Curtis, an equally gifted copywriter. "Hi, M. J., hello Ginny. You guys haven't changed a bit in five years . . . please say I haven't either."

A ripple of nervous laughter. The group had been affected by the news they heard downstairs. Who wouldn't? I echoed Cunningham's final words in the lobby, telling the group that I shared his faith in their ability to create a campaign that would keep the account at Adams & Benson.

"Now let's get the introductions out of the way. I met Matt and Manny this morning, and I've read your personnel files. Help me match names with faces."

"Sure," said the attractive African-American woman sitting with M.J. and Ginny. "Gloria Johnson. Been here about three years. Came from Campbell-Ewald . . . I was senior art director on Chevy mid-size."

"Liked your work there, Gloria," I said. "Especially that Chevy 'Malibu at Malibu' ad."

"Aw, call her Glo-Jo," drawled the man in the cowboy hat. "Everybody else does."

Pickard and Glo-Jo Johnson were one of the company's premier writer-art director teams, and by far the most unlikely. He was a slim, blonde Texan with a slow drawl, she an outgoing black woman who had grown up on Detroit's west side. They had experienced a love-hate relationship from the start: Bob Roy loved Glo-Jo with all his heart; she wanted nothing to do with him.

But it soon became obvious that their relationship, while not made in heaven, just might have been conceived in the advertising hall of fame. Alone, both had been solid creative talents. Together, much to Glo-Jo's chagrin, they were dynamite, their work copping awards in virtually every major advertising competition.

"By the way," said the man in the cowboy hat, "I'm Bob Roy Pickard. I was driving cars before I could write about 'em."

"Some people would say that's still true," said Glo-Jo.

I looked over at the young man at the table with the three women, the one who looked like he still attended high school.

"Will Parkins," the kid said quickly, sitting up straight. "Graduated from the school of art at Columbia in June. And . . . and I hope to be here a lot longer."

"You will be, Will. Just give us the best you have, and we'll all be fine.

"It's nearly time to meet with Cunningham and Higgins. Let's get to the eighth floor conference room and find out what the hell this is all about."

15

Now

We drove into Gaylord's small downtown, its Main Street lined with brightly painted shops and restaurants. The day was warm and sunny, people walked the sidewalks in shorts and short-sleeved shirts. I found it puzzling to see a number of men walking in groups of four, until Higgins pointed out the popularity of the Gaylord area with golfers. A dozen courses lay within a short putt of the downtown area.

Higgins parked the Avatar AVX on a side street and we did our shopping quickly, picking up clothes and food. No one seemed to recognize our faces; something I feared would change once Detroit papers hit the Northern Michigan newsstands. The killing of the policeman and our "escape" would rate front-page coverage, complete with photos of Sean and me.

I kept thinking about the people back at Adams & Benson: co-workers like Matt Carter, Will Parkins, M.J., Glo-Jo and Bob Roy. And Manny . . . poor Manny. Would they trust we were innocent of murdering that policeman, or would they believe Bacalla's story? I remembered what Paul Chapman had said about Bacalla at lunch that day, how he hardly knew the man even after working with him for months, and hoped our co-workers were all giving us the benefit of the doubt.

We left downtown with enough food for ten days if we ate sparingly, a week if we didn't. We could stay out of sight that long at Higgins' cottage.

But what then?

16

Monday, Oct. 11–3:59 p.m.

Baron Nichols and his group were already in the conference room, all eight along one side of the long oak conference table. We took seats on the opposite side. Cunningham and Higgins hadn't yet arrived.

The scene reminded me of a seventh grade dance where the girls huddled together on one side of the room, the boys on the other. Normally, there would have been conversation, a bit of light-hearted bantering, but the news of Cato's death and the announcement in the lobby created a tension that reached into the pits of our stomachs. Each person gazed nervously about the room, trying to avoid the eyes of others.

I didn't mind the silence. Nichols' actions at lunch still galled me. If our groups had to compete, bring it on.

I found myself daydreaming, gazing out the expansive floor-to-ceiling window with its view of the downtown skyline. I pictured King Kong on top of the Penobscot Building, F-16 fighters circling the building. Instead of Fay Wray or Jessica Lange, the big ape had Baron Nichols clenched in one gigantic fist.

The vision kept getting better; Mr. Kong was about to discover how high Nichols would bounce off Woodward Avenue when Ken Cunningham entered with a well-groomed, sandy-haired man in his mid-thirties I knew must be Sean Higgins, and an assistant account executive whose name I learned was Lyle Windemere.

I chalked off Windemere immediately as the typical young, butt-kissing account assistant. As for Higgins, my first impression was that he looked a little *too* carefully groomed—an Armani suit that cost two grand if it cost a dime, a crisply starched white shirt and a hand-made Countess Mara necktie. *Probably the type who visited a barber twice a week.*

After introducing me to both men, Cunningham began. "I see everyone's here. Let me say that Darren Cato's death has certainly come as a shock. He was a fine producer.

"But I'm afraid we have to look beyond his passing for the moment. Because together, we face a crisis that threatens not only us, but dozens of our friends. We must create advertising that will win the business and keep the AVC account at Adams & Benson.

"Darcy, Baron. I've invited both of your groups to participate because we need to explore as many options as we can. You'll work independently and, in the end, just one of your campaigns will be presented."

"That's fine with us, Ken," Nichols said. "We welcome the competition."

Kiss my ass, Nichols. His flaming red hair had gotten him the nickname "Red Baron," but "Flaming Ass" seemed more like it.

Cunningham continued. "We've all read about the industry's attempts to perfect an electric vehicle that's acceptable to the American driving public.

"Until now the big hurdle has been range. The American consumer won't accept a car that can't travel farther than eighty or a hundred miles without recharging.

"Today we learned that, through one of its subsidiaries, American Vehicle has scored a major breakthrough . . . a fuel cell that gives their electric car a range of more than five hundred miles on a single charge."

That news bought a round of murmurs from both creative groups. Cunningham went on. "AVC's engineers say the car will perform like a conventionally-powered vehicle. Zero to sixty in the eight to nine second range."

"Why hasn't the press gotten wind of it?" Carter asked.

"AVC has gone to great lengths to keep this quiet. Not even their people know much about the new vehicle. We do know the vehicle is a small car. Seats four, max. But AVC isn't concerned with size . . . they see the market as singles and young marrieds without children.

"They want to stress the car's range, with quiet performance and inexpensive operation a close second and third.

"The first production models won't roll off the line for a month, but they want to break out the advertising campaign as soon as possible. They know the competition is close to developing their own long range vehicles, and they want the Ampere announced first."

"The Ampere?" This time it was Baron Nichols asking the question.

Before Cunningham could answer, Windemere jumped in. "That's the name their marketing people came up with, Baron," he said. "It did well in focus panels."

Cunningham shot Windemere a sideways glance. "Our mission," he continued, "is to develop a full-blown advertising campaign. I want to show our client comprehensive layouts, with copy and visuals just as they'll appear in newspapers and magazines. And I want to present a mocked-up TV commercial on DVD disc, complete with actor and announcer voices."

Higgins had been leaning back in his chair watching the reactions of the two creative groups. Now he turned to Cunningham. "You don't think they can visualize the commercial from story board images?"

"Those guys are engineers and numbers crunchers. They couldn't visualize a fart after three helpings of baked beans. I want to hit them right between the eyes.

"But there's another reason. Time is critical. The quicker we get them on the air, the better our chances of getting the business.

"The first prototype Ampere won't be available for filming for three weeks. That means the other two agencies probably won't plan to put them on air for at least a month and a half. But if we keep our TV ideas simple enough to produce with computer animation, we can be on air before that. We've just invested two million in the latest computer animation equipment. Let's make the most of it."

A few murmurs and groans sounded. The creative people on both teams were convinced their hands had been tied. While the writers, art directors and producers at the other two agencies would have free reign, they were being limited to what could be generated on computer.

"Look, I know you can do it," Cunningham said, trotting out the charm that endeared him to A & B clients. "No cast of thousands. No spectacular panoramic shots. Just the kind of bright ideas you folks have come up with time and time again."

"When do you present to AVC?" Nichols asked.

"Four weeks from today. Sean Higgins will be in charge of the project, assisted by Lyle Windemere." Windemere beamed at the sound of his name and I suspected he'd be wagging his tail if he had one.

"We'll be giving you more details on the car itself," Cunningham said. "All I can add are my wishes for your success in creating a campaign that will keep the business here at A & B.

"Any other questions?"

"Just the obvious," I said. "When do you and Higgins want to see our ideas in an internal presentation?"

"Yesterday."

17

5:43 p.m.

Work on the Ampere campaign began immediately. With the prospect of a long evening ahead, I decided to have supper for the group delivered to my office.

The team voted for Chow Ling's Chinese, but when the eight white paper bags arrived they might as well have contained Puppy Chow. Slumped in leather chairs and seated around the glass top table, the group picked at their meals like fussy third graders.

They were feeling the weight of a responsibility none had asked for. Hundreds of A & B employees and their families depended on the advertising we would create over the next few weeks.

That cloud might have hung over the group all evening if it hadn't been for Lyle Windemere. I hadn't known Windemere for more than a few hours, but I had him pretty well pegged: a self-important junior account executive whose duties consisted primarily of running errands for Sean Higgins. Red haired, freckled and fresh out of graduate school, he gave no outward indication of the slightest ability to rally the troops. In fact, it seemed a safe bet he couldn't inspire a group of weight watching dropouts with a pastry cart packed with cannoli.

Nonetheless suddenly there he stood, ramrod straight, clearing his throat as if about to deliver the State-of-the-Union address before Congress.

"First of all," he began, "let me thank each of you in advance for your fine efforts. I know you'll come up with something Ken, Sean and I will be proud of."

I heard a soft groan and saw Bob Roy Pickard's eyes roll back in his head. If Windemere noticed, he gave no sign.

"I was putting in a little O.T. myself," he said, "and decided to drop by and see what you've come up with."

What we'd come up with? Was he joking? We'd had the assignment less than four hours. The man clearly had no perception of the creative process or the people involved in it.

My group, on the other hand, knew exactly what to think of a stuffed shirt who walked around the agency as if he had a stick in his rear. I sat back and watched as Matt Carter pulled Windemere's chain.

"You got here right on time," Carter said. "We were just finishing up the campaign."

"You were?"

"Sure. We even decided on a name for the car."

"Ridiculous. If you'd listened to Ken Cunningham's briefing, you'd know they already have a name. Ampere."

"That's what I mean," Carter said. "AVC blew it."

Windemere stood with his arms folded. "I suppose you have a better name for an electric car?"

"Sure," Carter said. "Volts-wagon."

The humor flew over Windemere's head like an F-16. "Volkswagen? You can't be serious. That name's already taken."

Bob Roy Pickard jumped in. "Lyle, I want your opinion on a headline."

"Hit me with it."

"We want to convince people to take their electric vehicles back to an AVC dealer when they need service."

"Yes?"

"How about 'Let us look into your shorts'?"

"Very funny. Don't you creatives ever get serious?"

"I tried it once," Pickard said. "My ads all sounded like they were written by account executives."

More smiles, perhaps a chuckle or two. The mood of the group lifted. Observing these writers and art directors trading insults with Windemere was like watching a cat playing with a chipmunk it was about to devour. I decided to save Windemere from digging himself in any deeper.

"We appreciate your interest, Lyle," I said, smothering a laugh, "but the Ampere is a unique vehicle. Creating a campaign that does it justice is going to take a lot more time than we've had so far."

Windemere left in a huff, hands shoved deep in his pockets, shoulders hunched around his ears, completely clueless to the positive contribution his appearance had produced.

18

10:28 p.m.

As I drove to the two-story house in Detroit's Indian Village area the agency had provided as temporary quarters, my thoughts washed back over the evening.

I pictured Will, Ginny, Glo-Jo, Matt Carter and the others, and remembered how nervous they seemed at first over the challenge facing them. I remembered how that fear had disappeared, replaced by a determination to meet the challenge, to create a campaign that would win the AVC business and save not only their jobs, but the careers of their friends.

What about me? I thought. What about Jeff Luden? He offered me a job, with a pay raise of twenty grand.

Until this moment, I hadn't made time to consider the offer. Maybe it sounds crazy, but if we weren't in such a horrible mess the decision would have been a whole lot easier. A twenty thousand dollar pay raise was something even Ken Cunningham and Sid Goldman would understand if I decided to bail after one day on the job.

I hadn't asked for this situation: caught in an uphill fight with three agencies in a battle only one would win.

But I could choose what I would do about it.

I thought again of the looks on the faces in my office, and the gutsy resolve of the people who wore them. I'd never been a quitter, and no way could I justify running out on people who trusted me with their futures as well as their jobs.

The clock on the instrument panel read ten-thirty; nine-thirty in Chicago, early enough to call Jeff Luden.

To tell him I intended to stay and fight.

19

11:18 p.m.

Hello?

Hi, Dad.

Dad? Who's that calling me Dad? Do I have a daughter?

Sorry I haven't called till now, Dad. What with moving all my belongings and then finally starting work, the pace here has been absolutely unreal.

So you haven't forgotten us?

I've been running from the time I got to Detroit. And now we're crashing on a top-secret project I can't talk about. Today lasted 14 hours.

Can't talk about it, huh? Must be important.

Maybe too important. We have to re-pitch one of A & B's oldest accounts. If we lose the business, the agency's going to lose jobs.

That doesn't sound fair.

You taught me a long time ago that life isn't fair.

I read in the paper that a man was killed . . . a video editor. Did you know him?

I didn't, but some of the people I work with did. And later today we heard that one of our producers here at A & B was found dead.
Are you sure you're okay? I worry about you, Kitten.
I'll be fine, Dad. I'm all grown up now.
Watch your step. Anything can happen in a big city.
I'll be careful.
Have you seen Ken Cunningham?
Seen him? He's all over the place. He sends his regards, by the way.
Tell him I said hello. And get some sleep Kit. You sound tired.
I am Dad. I love you. And give my love to Melanie. I'll call soon.
I love you Kit. Goodnight.

20

Tuesday, Oct. 12 8:45 a.m.

I arrived at Adams & Benson surprised to find my former husband in the parking lot. Between the non-descript brown suit he wore and the non-descript blue Ford Taurus he emerged from, you'd have him pegged him as a cop from across the River. He saw me and nodded.

"What brings you back to Adams & Benson?" I asked.

"How well do you know a guy by the name of Sean Higgins?" Garry hadn't changed. He considered small talk something midgets engaged in.

"I met him yesterday. Why?"

"A couple people say Higgins and Cato were oil and water."

"So what? I thought the official report of Cato's death said suicide."

"We're treating it like homicide. The guy had plans with his girl friend for that evening," Garry said. "Not your typical suicide candidate. And he had sunglasses on when they found the body."

"What's that got to do with it?"

"Whoever killed him had a weird sense of humor. Sunglasses wouldn't have stayed on if he'd been thrashing at the end of a rope. The ME rushed through the autopsy and guess what? Cato died of a heart attack."

"From hanging?"

"He was dead before the rope touched his neck."

"But a heart attack . . ."

"There are poisons that can cause heart failure. The ME's looking into it."

"What makes Higgins a suspect?"

"They didn't get along, for one thing. And wasn't Higgins a football player?"

"He played for the University of Michigan."

"Cato wasn't exactly a lightweight. Whoever strung up his body after he died had to be strong."

* * *

When I got to my desk, a voice mail message said Higgins wanted to see me. I found him in his office, typing away at his computer with all the skill and dexterity two fingers could manage.

He kept his eyes on the keyboard as he spoke. "Welcome back to the big time. I hear you built quite a reputation here five years ago. Then ran away."

"It was more walk than run. I had to get away from Detroit for a while."

"I saw you talking to that cop down in the parking lot. Any more news on Cato?" Apparently Higgins shared Kaminski's distaste for chit-chat.

"That cop is my former husband; the reason I had to get away from Detroit. He says Cato's death was murder, not suicide."

"Murder, huh? I thought they found him hanged."

"Yeah. Wearing sunglasses. The police figure they would've fallen off if he'd actually hanged himself. But the clincher is, the Medical Examiner's report says he died of a heart attack. Someone strung him up to make it look like suicide."

Higgins stopped typing and looked up. "Is that it?"

"Not quite. He asked if I knew you."

"So I'm a suspect?"

"For what it's worth, I told him I didn't think you did it. But he heard you and Cato didn't get along."

"If I had killed him, they would have found those sunglasses up his butt."

"The man's dead. Remind me to nominate you for the Mr. Sensitivity Award."

* * *

Higgins apologized. Not for the crass remark, but for interfering with work on the Ampere. He said we had to divert at least one team to create an Avion print ad for the first issue of *Self* magazine we could make. He gave me the input, and I called Glo-Jo and Bob Roy.

They were waiting in my office when I got there. After passing on Higgins' apology, I relayed the information he'd provided.

"So the object is to convey a younger, racier image for the Avion," Glo-Jo said as I finished.

"Yep. Not exactly a snap. Research says most people consider Avion a car for the geriatric set."

"No problem. I know just what to do," said Pickard.

"Great," said Glo-Jo. "What is it?"

"Simple. We use subliminal persuasion."

Glo-Jo raised an eyebrow. "We use what?"

"Subliminal. Remember that movie theatre experiment where that guy flashed 'you're thirsty' on the screen too fast for the conscious mind to see and soda pop sales shot through the roof? And where some art director retouched s-e-x in the ice cubes in a liquor ad to attract readers."

Glo-Jo tried to decide whether to take him seriously. "Yeah, so what?"

"Don't you get it? We retouch the words 'buy an Avion' lightly in the paint of the car in our ad. Readers see the words subliminally and buy an Avion without ever having a conscious thought about it."

"I don't think anyone who believes that BS would ever have a conscious thought about anything," Glo-Jo sniffed.

"*Some* people fall for it, Darlin'. Hey, the guy who wrote the book about that liquor ad made a fortune."

Glo-Jo turned to me. "What's your take on that subliminal stuff, Darcy?"

"I'm with you, Glo-Jo. I read where someone challenged the man to repeat the movie theatre experiment and he came up empty-handed. But whether you believe in it or not, it's still illegal. "So you'd better get to work on the real thing. Higgins is expecting an Avion ad by five o'clock."

21

4:58 p.m.

Higgins lined up a putt into the electronic ball return as I strolled into his office carrying Glo-Jo's ad layout.

I handed Higgins the layout and he stood motionless, staring at it. Finally he looked up.

"The headline: *This pedal will test your mettle*. I just don't know."

"You wanted a headline that grabbed attention," I said.

"Yes, but . . ."

"*This pedal will test your mettle*. Don't you get it?"

"I get it," Higgins said. "But I think it goes a little too far."

"Too far?" How could the man back down from the direction he had given me just that morning? "What kind of headline would you suggest?"

"The headline on our last ad was: *The family car that didn't forget the family.*"

"The family car that didn't forget the family? What the hell kind of headline is that?"

"You think it's dull?"

"Dull? That ad should carry a warning label against operating heavy machinery while reading it."

Higgins looked at the layout again. "I just think this ad is too strong."

"How about letting the client judge?"

"Okay, but give me an alternate. When this one goes up in flames, I want something to fall back on besides my ass."

"I'll write one. If you stick around, I'll have it for you by six. But promise me you'll show him this ad first."

Higgins gave the layout one more look. "Yeah, sure."

I walked out hoping Higgins was a man of his word.

* * *

Next morning, I found Higgins at his office closet, carefully placing a blue blazer on a hanger.

"Just got back from the breakfast meeting." He smoothed the blazer with his free hand. "Your pedal, mettle ad hit the rocks."

"Don't tell me," I said, "Murphy didn't get it."

"He got it. He just doesn't think the public will."

"Apparently Murphy doesn't give the public credit for having intelligence. He wants to spoon feed information . . . and that makes for dull ads."

"Don't get upset. He loved the other ad you wrote."

"That's not the point. I wrote that ad to give Murphy a choice. It's nowhere near as good as the one Bob Roy wrote."

"Well that's the one the client's going with."

"Let me see that ad . . . the second one."

Higgins reached into the briefcase on his desk and retrieved the layout. I took it and scanned the copy.

"What's the matter?" Higgins asked.

"I wrote this last night with one eye on the clock. Maybe I can't change the headline, but I can make damn sure the copy is the best I can write. Let me brighten it up. I promise not to make any drastic changes that'll give Murphy a coronary."

"Let me get this straight. Murphy bought your ad . . . and you're unhappy?"

"That's right."

"I don't get it."

I left Higgins scratching his head.

22

Wednesday, Oct. 13—Noon

No one needed a watch to pinpoint high noon at Big Norm's. The crowded dining area and the line at Willis' maitre'd stand were as telling as any timepiece.

Ken Cunningham had suggested the lunch. When he heard of our mild disagreement over the Avion ad, he called Higgins and me into his office like a couple of quarreling school kids. He explained we had to work together now more than ever; he would be out of town frequently during the coming weeks. The agency's major accounts needed assurance that the Adams & Benson Advertising Agency was solid enough to withstand the loss of the American Vehicle Corporation business, if it came. He recommended a peace-making lunch, on him.

Ken was right, of course. I decided to try my best to convince Higgins I didn't consider him a tasteless bore. With a smile as wide as it was phony, I made small talk while we waited for a table.

"Until I was here the other day, I'd forgotten how much I missed Detroit's restaurants," I said as we finally got to our table.

"What convinced you to come back?" Higgins asked. "The challenge . . . money?" He seemed to be trying, too.

"Neither, really. It was just time to face the fact that my marriage has been over nearly five years."

Finding the topic uncomfortable, I shifted gears. "What about you? What brought you to the Motor City?"

"I was born here. Grew up twenty miles from downtown Detroit, in Royal Oak. Went to Brother Rice High School."

"And played football?"

"It put me through college. But I studied too." He added the last almost defensively. "My parents made sure both my sister and I hit the books hard."

"You have a sister?"

"Patricia." Higgins paused, then: "She and Darren Cato were engaged."

"Darren Cato?"

Higgins must have noticed the surprise in my voice. He hesitated, but knew he had gone too far to stop. "Turned out Cato wasn't really serious. He broke the engagement and it took Pat months to get over him. She admitted later that she cried almost every night."

"I can empathize. My marriage wasn't exactly a walk in the park."

"Yeah, well, the hell of it is, I introduced them. Pat's married now, with a couple of nice kids. But I never forgave Cato for the pain he caused.

"That's where that remark about Cato's sunglasses and a certain orifice of his body came from," Higgins said. The hint of a smile curled the corners of his mouth. "I just want you to know that I'm not entirely insensitive."

With that, he picked up one of the two menus in front of him and handed it to me.

"I can recommend the seafood. The catch of the day is always fresh."

A waiter appeared, reeled in two orders of broiled pickerel, the catch du jour, and headed for the kitchen. As our conversation continued, I actually found myself enjoying Higgins' company. For a moment I thought, maybe just maybe, I had misjudged him. But then, like a jaguar lurking in the brush, he steered the conversation back to the AVC account.

"Okay, let's talk shop for a minute," he said. "It's important we reach an understanding on a couple of points."

"Shoot." *Shoot?* I felt like shooting him. I could feel this conversation taking on the tone of a one-sided lecture.

"As you noticed on your 'pedal mettle' ad, our client John Murphy is pretty conservative."

Conservative? How about afraid of his own shadow? "But what if a concept that seems out of the ordinary sells cars?" I asked.

"Murphy's not about to take chances because some offbeat approach might win your group an award for so-called creativity."

That did it. The suggestion that I'd choose personal glory over selling a client's product was pure BS. "I'm not talking about awards," I shot back. "You know damn well the most effective advertising is created when rules are broken."

"Not as long as I run the AVC account."

"You may run the account, but I've been hired to create the advertising. I can't do it if you tie my hands."

I bit my tongue as the waiter arrived with our meals. He might as well have left the food in the kitchen; my appetite had vanished. The argument hadn't put a dent in Higgins' appetite. Fork in one hand, knife in the other, the jerk made like a dust-hungry Hoover.

I decided to try one more time. "Why not let the client decide, instead of dictating what you'll show him?"

Higgins took another bite. "I don't want you wasting time on ads that never see the light of day."

"I'm more than happy to take the risk."

"Easy for you. You don't have to account for expenses. Your little creative group gets paid whether they spend time on solid ideas or mental masturbation."

Little creative group? Mental masturbation?

"Look, Higgins, you run the business part of the account." Now on my feet, I threw the napkin on the table. "But Ken Cunningham hired me to run the creative. Let's leave it to him. If he thinks I'm not cutting it, he can damn well assign me somewhere else. Is that clear?"

I stormed from the restaurant knowing that if Higgins had his way, that reassignment would have me sorting mail the rest of my career.

23

12:31 p.m.

Back at the agency, I found the lobby deserted except for Marlene, the friendly brunette at the receptionist's desk. Even the second and third floor offices overlooking the huge arena were vacant.

My security key opened the elevator door on the sixth floor. Stepping into the hallway I nearly got bowled over by a large man in a business suit carrying a briefcase and doing a hell of an impression of a run-away water buffalo.

"Hey, watch it!" I peppered him with a few epithets questioning his ancestry, but stopped when I realized my words bounced off him like I had. He just kept speed walking toward the VanBuhler side of the floor. I realized then he had had a strong odor of alcohol about him, whiskey probably.

As I watched him disappear around the curve of the hallway, my anger changed to suspicion. What the hell was a stranger doing on the sixth floor?

* * *

My suspicions leaped a giant step forward when Matt Carter called.

"Darcy, the Avion submaster is missing."

"You're kidding."

"I had the DVD hidden in my credenza under a couple of Ampere layouts. I've asked everyone. No one's seen it."

I told Carter about my encounter with the heavyset man. Since the floor was off limits to anyone without a key, he had to be a prime suspect.

"Let's pay the VanBuhler team a visit," Carter said.

I considered the idea, but thought better of it. "We'll sure look stupid if we're wrong."

Then I got an idea myself. I called Paul Chapman, describing the buffalo who nearly ran me over in the hallway.

Chapman recognized him. "J. R. Roland. Started yesterday. He's another of those VanBuhler guys from D. C."

"Why would he be on our side of the sixth floor?"

"Maybe he got lost."

Maybe. But what about the disappearing DVD? I decided it might be wise to visit VanBuhler headquarters after all.

24

5:55 p.m.

My Ampere creative team would be working well into the night, but the VanBuhler people were a different story. By five-thirty you could fire a cannon through their side of the building without hitting anyone.

If I were going to explore enemy territory, now was the time. I walked out into the corridor, moving slowly toward the elevators that divided the two sides of the floor. I paused there, facing the doors as if waiting for the next car. I glanced to my right, down the carpeted corridor toward the offices of the VanBuhler staff.

The hallway proved deserted, so I made my move, walking quickly to the right. A couple of butterflies were playing chicken in my stomach; I was entering an area off-limits to everyone but VanBuhler staffers. What would happen if I were caught?

Would I be fired? Probably not. At this point, I was too valuable to the agency. But there would be a severe reprimand, not to mention the sheer embarrassment.

I saw people in very few of the offices I passed, and fortunately they were too intent on their work to notice me. As I walked, I read the names of office occupants printed on cards inside metal frames at the right of each door. I had no idea where Roland's office was, but prayed I'd find it soon—and empty.

Passing the fifth door, I saw Roland's name just ahead. I strolled past the open door, sneaking a glance inside.

Empty.

I walked back and peered in. The far wall was a floor-to-ceiling window looking out over Jefferson Avenue winding its way east. A simple metal desk sat to the right of the door, nothing on it. Bare walls added to the Spartan appearance.

I darted inside. The search took seconds: three drawers on the right of Roland's desk, a large flat one in the front. I found a half empty fifth of whiskey in the bottom drawer, aside from that, nothing. Not a pencil, a pen, not even a paper clip. Roland traveled light.

If the DVD wasn't here, where was it? Maybe Roland passed it on to Robert Bacalla, the man Chapman said was in charge of the VanBuhler group. Back in the hallway, I decided to delve further into VanBuhler country. As I approached the office two doors down, I noticed the card outside the door read, "R. M. Bacalla." Was he in? My heart beat faster, the butterflies in my stomach now doing somersaults. The door stood wide open; I decided to reprise my tactic of walking by and glancing in without stopping.

The office proved empty. I turned back and went in. The room seemed twice the size of Roland's, and from the leather chairs and sofa to the colorful prints on the walls, it had been luxuriously furnished. The view of Jefferson Avenue from the floor-to-ceiling window behind the large oak desk mirrored the scene from Roland's office.

I noticed a closet to my left, door ajar. Approaching it, I heard voices in the hallway. Two men. What if they came in? I opened the closet door and slipped inside, pulling it shut behind me. In the darkness I heard the voices growing louder, then trailing off.

I opened the door a crack and looked around.

No one.

My pulse racing, I pushed the door open. As the inside of the closet lightened, I noticed a leather holster on a belt hanging from a hook to my left. I removed the belt and holster from the hook, unsnapped the flap on top of the holster, and looked inside.

Empty.

"Looking for this?"

Startled by the deep masculine voice, I spun around. Facing me stood a tall, dark-complected man with a thin mustache. *Holding a pistol.* The shock was only momentary. Then, surprise turned to anger. This, obviously, was Robert Bacalla, and while I didn't have an explanation for being in his office, he certainly had no business carrying a gun inside the building.

"No, I'm looking for answers," I said, trying to project more confidence than I felt. "What right do you have bringing a gun into this building?"

The man had been pointing the pistol toward me. Now he lowered the barrel, and transferred the weapon to his left hand where it appeared less threatening.

"I have a permit. I occasionally carry campaign funds for the election committee. Sometimes a hundred thousand or more dollars. This pistol is the committee's idea."

He spoke in the precise fashion of someone to whom English is a second language.

"Now, it is my turn to ask a question. What is your business on this side of the sixth floor?"

"I . . . I guess I was curious." The words sounded weak, even to me. "I work here on six . . . on the AVC account."

"But you realize, do you not, this part of the floor is off-limits to anyone not working for me?"

"Yes. Yes, I do." I felt humiliated standing there, having to take this like a child caught smoking. Turning to leave, I saw a DVD in a clear plastic case on the coffee table in front of the sofa. As I read the words "Avion submaster" through the case, I suddenly felt stronger.

"Actually, I was looking for this." I snatched up the disc. "It's the submaster copy of an Avion commercial my group needs. It was stolen." I looked directly into Bacalla's eyes. "And I thought it might be here."

"Take it," Bacalla said with a wave of his hand. "One of my people found it in the elevator. I have no need for it."

"Thank you." I headed for the door. I couldn't get away fast enough.

"And please stay on your side of the building."

On the trip back to my office I vowed I'd find a way to wipe the damn smirk off Bacalla's face.

25

6:32 p.m.

The anger I felt leaving Bacalla magnified a hundredfold by the time I reached my office and found Sean Higgins standing by my desk.

"Darcy, about lunch . . ."

Brushing past him, I slammed the DVD on my desk. "Son-of-a-bitch," I hissed.

"Damn it, Darcy, I came here to apologize. I don't deserve that."

I blinked a couple of times, took a deep breath and came back down to earth. "Sorry. It's not you. It's Bacalla."

"Bacalla?"

"Robert M. Bacalla, head of the frigging VanBuhler group. The son-of-a-bitch had this stolen Avion submaster in his office; then made me feel like a trespasser when I went to get it.

"There's something strange going on here." Starting at the beginning, I told Higgins about the gun, the missing DVD, and the lecture from Bacalla that left me chewing nails.

"But why would they want that Avion DVD?"

I had thought about that. "Maybe Roland didn't know it was an Avion DVD."

"What do you mean?"

"Carter said it was in his credenza. With his Ampere materials."

"So?"

"What if Roland thought the DVD had something to do with the Ampere campaign? There could have been a sample Ampere TV commercial on it. The kind we put together in the Media Center."

"But you said it's clearly labeled 'Avion submaster.'"

"So maybe we mislabeled the disc to throw off anyone who might want to steal it."

"You're overlooking one thing, Darcy. Bacalla and his people are focused on getting VanBuhler elected. What do they care about the Ampere?"

I wasn't certain myself, but Higgins' mind seemed closed to any idea outside the ordinary. "I'm sure they want to see VanBuhler elected. But what if one of them—Roland, say—is also working for one of the agencies we're competing against for the AVC business?"

Higgins exhaled. "Okay, okay. Anything's possible. But it's obvious to me Carter left the disc on the elevator and is afraid to admit it. One of Bacalla's people found it, just as he said."

It sounded like BS to me, but before I could say so, Higgins turned to leave.

"I'm glad your imagination is working," he said over his shoulder. "But try to keep it focused on the Ampere."

26

11:14 p.m.

Hello?

Dad, it's me.

Kit! How are things in the Motor City?

They're great, advertising wise.

What do you mean?

The campaign we're working on is coming along well.

Then why the hesitation in your voice?

Dad, there's something going on here I don't like. Something besides the two murders I mentioned the last time we talked.

What do you mean, Kit?

I wish I knew. There are some people I'm convinced are up to something, but I'm not sure what it is.

Your hunches have always been good.

That's just it. I wish I had a stronger hunch.

What's your guess?

I think they might be working for another agency, one of the companies we're pitching against. They may be trying to get information on that campaign we're crashing.

Industrial spies?

Something like that.

Kit, you be careful.

I am, Dad. I go home after work every night.

I hope you find some time to enjoy yourself.

I haven't gotten out at all. But I've been playing a little Gershwin on the piano. It helps me relax.

You have a piano?

Yes, and what a surprise. It came with the house the agency found me in Indian Village.

Indian Village? What did they find you, a teepee?

No. Indian Village is a small community on the east side of Detroit. Mainly professional people. The homes are older. Mine was built in the Twenties.

And it's still standing?

The homes are older, but they're kept up very well. Like a certain gentleman I know.

Hey, I'm not that old. At least Melanie doesn't think so.

How's Melanie doing?

She sends her love. And I hear her calling. It's time for bed.

Tired already, Dad?

Who said anything about sleeping?

Don't ever change, Dad. I love you.

I love you, too, Kit. Goodnight.

27

Now

It was nearly noon when Higgins finally found the dirt road that led to his uncle's cabin. We drove down a narrow trail past a number of cottages boarded up for the winter. Higgins explained the majority of the lake's residents were seasonal.

It occurred to me that we were isolated from ninety-nine percent of the state's population, and my ex-husband's warning came back to me. I didn't know Higgins well, but I felt certain he was incapable of murdering Darren Cato, no matter how much he disliked him. I tucked the thought away.

As the Avatar pulled into a sandy drive bordered by pines on both sides, I found myself facing the back of a small, red aluminum-sided cottage with a gray shingled roof and an attached garage. It lay among a grove of oak, birch and northern pine, and through the trees I saw the bright blue waters of a lake.

Higgins found a key under the porch. Carrying large grocery bags in each arm, I followed him through the back door, through a bedroom and into the living area of the cottage. Higgins opened the blinds covering the front window, and revealed a picturesque view of Lake Manuka. Vibrantly colored cottages ringed the far side a half-mile or so across. The quiet beauty reminded me of a Worthington Whittredge landscape.

The living room featured comfortable furniture, chosen for utility rather than decoration. A huge stone fireplace nearly covered the wall to my right, its blackened interior evidence of crackling wood fires on cool evenings past.

The cottage was rectangular, three bedrooms and a bathroom taking up the back half. The front comprised a living room, dining area and kitchen.

I set the grocery bags on the kitchen counter. Through a window over the sink I saw a white cottage on the lot next door, just beyond a clump of pines. An elderly woman raked leaves in the yard. Higgins saw me staring and walked over.

"I'll be damned," he said, "Mrs. Gordon is still alive."

"She looks ninety years old."

"She looked ninety years old when I was a teenager. She and her husband must have moved in just after the glaciers that dug these lakes receded. Mr. Gordon used to take me squirrel hunting."

He smiled. "You had to be a great shot to hunt with him."

"Why was that?"

"His rifles were both single-shot twenty-twos. If you missed, the squirrel was in the next county before you could reload." Higgins rubbed his stomach. "Enough history. Let's unload the car and eat."

I followed him outside. It was warm for a Michigan October, in the high sixties. Indian summer. I kicked off my shoes and enjoyed the feeling of cool, sandy soil oozing between my toes. A gentle breeze blew off the lake, rattling dry leaves clinging to branches overhead. An outboard motor purred somewhere.

I carried two bags filled with clothes into the corner bedroom. Returning to the back porch, I saw Higgins back a faded blue Chevrolet Lumina out of the garage into the sandy area behind. He replaced it with the Avatar and closed the door.

"If we go anywhere, this old Lumina is going to attract a lot less attention than the Avatar."

We carried the last of the grocery bags into the cabin and I went into the bedroom to unpack. When I came out, I found Higgins standing over a frying pan.

"How do you like your burgers?"

"Right now, I'd eat them raw."

We ate on the wooden deck in front of the cottage beneath a sky of brilliant blue, bothered only by an occasional cloud. A light October breeze stirred up small ripples on the lake, and brought the pleasant aroma of burning leaves from Mrs. Gordon's lot. But it wasn't long before the conversation drifted back to Detroit.

Higgins looked at his watch. "Two-thirty. The Ampere pitch should be over. Let's call the agency and see if there's any news."

"Speaking of news, how do you think they're taking the news about us and that policeman being shot?"

"You don't think anyone there actually believes we're guilty?"

"I just think we have to be careful who we talk to." "How about Ken Cunningham?"

"I trust him."

"So do I. Let's call."

But both phones, in the kitchen and my bedroom, were dead. "Turned off for the winter," Higgins said. "I should have thought of that."

"What now?"

"I'll go next door... use Mrs. Gordon's phone to call Cunningham, then call the phone company to get ours turned on."

I watched Higgins through the window over the sink. He approached Mrs. Gordon, talked for a moment, then went into her cottage. He was back in ten minutes.

"Cunningham said AVC management loved our presentation. But he doesn't expect a decision from AVC until at least tomorrow. Apparently the other two agencies are presenting in the morning."

"What did he say about our situation?"

"He still thinks we ought to give ourselves up. But he's not going to tip the authorities. He's taking a chance, you know."

I felt relieved... with both Ken's reaction and AVC's acceptance of our magazine ads and TV commercial. But the reality of our situation couldn't be denied: Even if we won the business, we'd be doing our jobs from behind bars if we didn't get out of this mess.

28

Thursday, Oct. 14—11:00 a.m.

The morning began with a message that Ken Cunningham wanted to see what our creative team had accomplished so far. The request seemed highly unfair after just two and a half days of work. But at eleven a.m. Team Ampere streamed into the eighth floor conference room with layouts, print copy and a television story board–all in their most embryonic stages. Cunningham, Higgins and Lyle Windemere sat around the large mahogany table. Cunningham didn't waste time.

"Thanks for coming. I apologize for interrupting your work with this impromptu meeting. But the reason will become obvious.

"First, we—Sean, Lyle and I—would like to see what you've done so far."

"Ken, we've just..." I cut my protest short as Cunningham raised his hand.

"Believe me, I know you've had no time at all. I merely want to see where we stand."

For the next few minutes I offered a capsulated version of the concepts the group had created. Cunningham seemed pleased.

"I like your thinking," he said. "And your plans for the Internet are right on target. But my main concern is television. How are you doing there?"

"I think we've come up with a pretty decent approach." Then, looking directly at Cunningham: "Given the limitations."

"I know I've limited your alternatives. But you'll understand in a moment. Let's see what you have."

I turned the floor over to Stankowski, Carter and Rodriguez, who ran through their television concept.

In the end, Cunningham was smiling. "I like it," he said. "How long will it take to get it ready to air?"

Carter started thinking out loud: "Computer animation... recording music... videotaping singers... I'd say three, four weeks."

"Can it be done faster? Say a week and a half?"

Carter whistled. "You're talking a ton of overtime and money, Ken. But sure, it can be done."

Cunningham leaned forward, elbows on the table. He lowered his voice. "Okay. Here's why I called this meeting.

"AVC isn't expecting anything for three weeks. And, until I saw your ideas, I figured we'd have to stick to that schedule. Sean and I reviewed Baron Nichols' group earlier and, frankly, they're nowhere near as far along as you are."

I couldn't help smiling. Winning the AVC business couldn't possibly feel any better than showing up Baron Nichols.

"Because of what I see here," Cunningham said. "I'm going to call Bill Kesler this morning and tell him we want to present our campaign early. Next Monday."

Next Monday? I couldn't believe my ears.

"Ken you can't be serious."

"Serious enough to gamble the entire American Vehicle account. Look, as it stands we have one chance in three of winning the business. That's not good enough. I'm a firm believer that when the odds aren't in your favor, change the game.

"Here's my plan: on October 25, exactly a week and a half from now, the New York Jets play the San Francisco Forty-Niners on ESPN's Monday Night Football."

"That's going to be a hell of a shoot out," Bob Roy said. "A rematch of last season's Super Bowl teams."

"Exactly," said Cunningham. "And the Super Bowl ended on a disputed call in overtime."

"The build-up for this game has been huge," Higgins said. "You're talking a Super Bowl size TV audience."

"Right," said Cunningham. "AVC's a regular sponsor; the people over there are beside themselves. They own two prime spots during the game, and that's the reason for this meeting. I'm going to roll the dice."

I looked over at Higgins. The slight smile curling his lips said he knew what was coming.

"AVC plans to run its usual Avion spots on that Monday night, ten days from now," Cunningham said. "But we're going to surprise them.

"I'm going to guarantee we can put them on air with the Ampere."

* * *

The meeting had been a two-edged sword.

Beating out Baron Nichols gave me more satisfaction than I wanted to admit. But Cunningham's move left me with an antsy feeling. It was gutsy, all right, but also reckless.

It reminded me of "Tonk," a card game I played as a child. Everyone started with three cards and continued to draw and discard, until someone thought he or she had the best hand. That player would "tonk," knock on the table. The others then drew a final card, and laid down their hands. The highest three cards won.

Once in a great while a player would refuse to draw any cards, tonking immediately after the deal, gambling his original three cards would be good enough to win.

Ken Cunningham seemed to be playing that game now—calling in the cards, betting that his company's campaign, as it now stood, would beat anything the other two agencies were holding. He was forcing their hands by readying A & B's Ampere commercial in time for the year's biggest television audience.

If right, A & B would keep its current AVC business, and rake in another nine hundred million in billings.

If wrong, the agency's largest account, one it had held more than ninety years, would be lost.

And with it, a few hundred jobs.

29

2:47 p.m.

I was filling in start times and due dates on the chart in my PC that inventoried the group's print and television ads when the phone on my desk rang.

"James."

"Miss James, this is Marsha Tower, Mr. Rathmore's administrative assistant." Her voice had a curt, take no prisoners quality.

Her formal tone didn't intimidate me. "Yes, Marsha?"

"Mr. Rathmore wants to see you. He asks that you be in his office at three o'clock. Sharp."

A click sounded at the other end of the line.

* * *

Marsha Tower turned out to be a trim blonde in her late fifties with a carefully manicured coiffure.

"Mr. Rathmore is meeting with Mr. Adams," she said, ushering me into the office of A & B's Board Chairman. "He'll return shortly. You may wait here."

Left alone, I looked around Rathmore's spacious office. Through the full-length window that made up the far wall, I could see east, past Belle Isle and almost to Lake St. Clair. To the right, across the River, lay southern Ontario.

Against the wall on my left, a long table held a variety of artifacts, carvings of stone and wood. I picked up what appeared to be a warrior chiseled out of stone.

"That's a Mayan chief," came a voice from behind me. "It's at least a thousand years old. Please don't drop it."

Surprised, I spun around, lucky I didn't drop the damn thing. C. J. Rathmore was about my height, five-feet-nine or so, dressed in a black suit, white shirt and red and black striped tie. He wore glasses with rimless, round lenses and had a rather dark complexion for an Englishman; still, the accent was unmistakably British.

I carefully set the figure back on the table. Rathmore had caught me off guard. "I . . . I'm sorry," I managed to stammer. "I didn't know."

"Of course you didn't. Otherwise you wouldn't have handled it."

So much for pleasant greetings.

"Please sit down." Rathmore motioned to one of three dark leather chairs.

"That carving is a ritual figure," Rathmore said, perhaps trying to make up for his initial harshness. "It's from the island of Jaina, off the coast of Campeche, Mexico. The Mayas used the island as a burial place for nobles between six and nine hundred A. D."

"Interesting," I said, wishing he would get to the point of this meeting.

"My mother was a descendant of the Mayas; my father, a British archeologist. They met in Mexico City while he was studying the Otomi paper makers of San Pablito, northeast of the City. They moved to London shortly before my birth."

"You seem to have inherited your father's interest in archeology."

"It's merely a hobby with me, I'm afraid." Rathmore paused. "I understand you have a hobby, too, Miss James. An unfortunate one."

"What do you mean?"

"You seem to fancy yourself a detective. What other reason would you have for trespassing into a secure area?"

"If you mean the VanBuhler side of the sixth floor, I had a good reason for being there. I was looking for a stolen DVD. I found it in Mr. Bacalla's office."

"Mr. Bacalla says one of his people discovered the disc on the lift."

"The lift?"

"The elevator."

"That was his story."

Rathmore threw up his hands. "I know very little about your DVD or how it got to Mr. Bacalla, Miss James. But I do know profit and loss statements. With the American Vehicle business in jeopardy, the VanBuhler account is more vital to this agency than ever. We cannot afford to lose it."

"Mr. Rathmore, I have no intention of jeopardizing this company's standing with Niles VanBuhler's people."

"Please see that you don't. I've seen your personnel file, Miss James, it's very impressive. It would be a pity to terminate someone with your talent over a matter like this."

Rathmore stood. The meeting had ended.

30

8:42 p.m.

The lonely baritone of a freighter's horn rolled through the fog, down the Detroit River. I heard it over the echoing click of my heels on the pavement of A & B's parking lot.

Strolling toward my car, I replayed the day's achievements. In spite of my run-in with Rathmore, I felt good. The Ampere commercial was on disc, layouts mounted on boards. Tomorrow we would rehearse for Saturday's presentation to Cunningham, Adams, Rathmore and Higgins. Matt, Manny and the others had left earlier, but I stayed to write the outline for our dog and pony show for A & B management.

The Detroit River reminded me of a song I loved to play on the piano: "Old Man River" from *Showboat*. Like the Mississippi, this was a blue-collar river, its waters the blood that carried nourishment to industrial facilities north and south. Coal in the bellies of northbound freighters fueled power plants in Marquette and Duluth. Southbound ships carried iron ore to steel mills in Ohio and Pennsylvania.

The A & B parking lot ran along the riverbank and I could hear waves licking the sea wall in the darkness to my left, where the light of the parking lot ended abruptly.

The lot was illuminated in circular patches of yellow that streamed from lights atop two rows of tall lampposts. Between the circles lay shadows of darkness. The temperature was mild, but a sudden rush of cool air blowing off the water sent a chill through me. My back to the building, I walked from light into darkness and back to light again, toward my car at the far end of the nearly empty lot.

The growl of an engine ripped through the fabric of my thoughts, a presence somewhere behind me. Startled, I whirled to see a car burst through the darkness, into a pool of light nearly a hundred feet away. Its headlights were off and it came at me fast.

I turned toward a light post fifteen feet to my left. If I could get there, it would shield me from the car. I ran, cursing the heels of my shoes. I lunged the last five feet, the car virtually on top of me. Its roar was deafening and I felt a rush of air as it sped by.

Tires squealed as the driver spun it around. It stopped about seventy feet from me, ahead and to my right.

There it sat, a black, ominous shape, half hidden in darkness. With the downtown lights in the background, I made out the silhouette of the driver waiting for my move. I wondered whether to stay behind the relative safety of the pole or to make a run for it. A tiny flash of light and a loud *pop* came from the direction of the car. I felt rather than heard something fly past, just over my head. *A bullet.*

I had to move. Another pole waited directly ahead, the distance about forty feet, but reaching it would put me closer to my car. I sensed the driver staring at me. I kicked off my shoes pulled my short skirt up around my waist and ran.

I heard the tires squeal and knew the race to the pole would be close. Maybe a photo finish. My heart beat wildly, my lungs burned for air. The pole loomed closer, but so did the car, a blur of motion to my right, its engine screaming. I made it to the pole as the car raced by, the driver braking hard, sliding almost to the riverbank.

I hugged the pole, breathing out of control, my vehicle another thirty feet straight ahead.

No time to rest.

I went for it, and heard tires squealing and an engine howling behind me.

I reached my car and fumbled for the key. The phantom car sped closer, engine shrieking. I felt the key, jammed it in the lock, opened the door and jumped inside. I pulled the door shut as the vehicle raced by. In another second it would have slammed into the door, crushing a leg or arm.

I stuffed the key into the ignition and twisted. As the engine started, I looked up to see the taillights of the phantom car race past the A & B Building, across Atwater Street and onto the short road leading to Jefferson Avenue.

Why had the driver given up so easily? The answer came from behind me as light flooded the interior of my car. In the rearview mirror I saw the headlights and silhouette of a security vehicle that had come into the A & B lot from the far entrance. With the dual lights on its roof, the car gave the appearance of a Detroit Police vehicle in the darkness. Police or security staff, it didn't matter.

I got out, waving at the vehicle. It rolled to a stop behind me.

"Help you, Miss?"

I struggled to catch my breath. "That car," I pointed toward Jefferson Avenue, "It tried to kill me."

"Which car?" The security officer squinted out toward the lights on Jefferson Avenue. By now whoever tried to run me down would be a mile away.

31

The patrolman and his partner arrived within five minutes of the security guard's call.

I had caught my breath, and calmed down somewhat.

"What was the make of the vehicle?"

I didn't have an answer. It was dark and everything happened so quickly I hadn't gotten a good look at the car or driver.

"Did you see the vehicle?" the second officer asked the security guard.

"Afraid not. When I drove back here on my round, the lot was deserted except for Ms. James. She got out of her car and waved me down. I called you. That's it."

"He had a gun," I said. "The man in the car shot at me."

"Where was the vehicle at the time the driver discharged his weapon?" the first cop asked.

I motioned to where the car had stopped. "Over there. I saw a flash, and I could feel the bullet go past and out there." I pointed at the river.

I walked the cops to the spot where the car had stood. The officers ran flashlight beams over the pavement for five minutes looking for a shell casing.

"Would there have to be one?" I asked.

"Not necessarily," the second cop said. "Not if the man had a revolver."

"How many shots?" asked the first cop.

"Just one."

"If there was a shot," he said, looking at his partner, "the bullet is at the bottom of the river."

"What do you mean, *if*? You think I'm making this up?" In a city the size of Detroit, with shootings every day, why was it so inconceivable that somebody might try to kill me?

"Are you sure it wasn't his car backfiring?" the first policeman asked.

"You're damn right I'm sure. The man fired a gun at me. What are you going to do about it?"

"Don't get excited, ma'am," the second officer said. "We're going to file a report. But you do realize that without a description of the driver or the vehicle, there's not much to go on."

I sat in the police car and tried to hold my temper as the cops asked more questions. With my life in danger, all they intended was to file a report. Worse, the driver got away. He missed this time, what about the next?

When the policemen figured they had enough answers, they walked me back to my car. I drove home alone, feeling a vulnerability brand new to me. I checked the rearview mirror constantly, watching for a car that might race up beside me . . . or one that might stay behind me too long.

The drive to Indian Village, just ten minutes from Adams & Benson, seemed to take forever. I stopped halfway up my driveway, directly opposite the side door of my house. I cut the engine, turned off the headlights and looked in every direction.

Was it possible that the man who tried to run me down knew where I lived? Had he followed me? Was he watching me now in the darkness, waiting to spring from behind my garage or one of the trees just a few feet from my car?

I pulled the key from the ignition and fumbled with the ring, finally locating the key to the side door. In one continuous motion I unlocked and opened the car door, swung out, jammed the key in the side door, opened it, slammed the car door, ran into the house, pulled that door shut and turned the bolt.

I left the interior lights off as I walked to the rear of my kitchen and peered out into the backyard. Bathed in moonlight, it looked empty. I double-checked the locks on front and back doors, then ran upstairs. I considered calling my father, but decided against it. I didn't want to worry him, and needed time to put tonight's happenings into perspective.

Feeling sweaty and dirty from running, I finally turned the bathroom light on, took a quick shower and went to bed. I hoped to doze off quickly, but it was well after three a.m. before I finally fell asleep.

32

Friday, Oct 15—9:27 a.m.

"What are the cops doing about last night?" Manny Rodriguez asked.

He, Matt Carter and I were having coffee at the table in my office.

I shrugged. "They filed a report. As far as I know, that's it."

The easy-going attitude was an act. I still hadn't gotten over last night, but I didn't want to burden the group with my anxiety and take their focus off the Ampere.

"Filed a report, huh? That's guaranteed to strike fear into the guy who tried to run you down," Rodriguez deadpanned.

"Too bad you didn't get the license number," Carter said. I shot him a look, and he realized how foolish his remark sounded. "Sorry."

I hadn't planned on telling anyone about the incident, but the night security guard told the man who relieved him, and the story had spread through the agency. Even so, I kept my suspicions about Bacalla, Roland and the Ampere campaign to myself. That too would create a diversion the group didn't need.

"What was the guy's motive?" Carter asked. "Why would anyone want to run you down?"

"Who knows? Look, I appreciate your concern. But for now, let the police worry about it."

"Doesn't sound like they're very worried," Rodriguez said.

"No, it doesn't. But let's leave the detective work to the cops and concentrate on creating advertising. And hope Ken Cunningham's strategy works."

* * *

Cunningham had asked for a final run through Saturday at three o'clock. I spent the rest of the day fine-tuning the presentation. All we lacked was an overall theme line.

"That's like saying the only thing the Titanic needed was an iceberg-proof hull," Bob Roy said. But by now the team was dragging after four straight twelve to fifteen hour days.

"I want all of you to go home and rest," I told them. "Come in fresh at ten sharp for the final push. We'll find a theme line that'll blow their socks off."

Rodriguez hung around after the others had gone.

"Planning on camping here tonight, Manny?"

"Nah. But I am going to stay awhile to work on that theme line."

"Be my guest." I had my briefcase in my hand. "Just turn out the lights when you leave."

"One more thing," Rodriguez said. "I borrowed that Avion submaster from Carter. I plan to give it a look on my Sony setup at home."

I gave him a thumbs up sign as I walked out the door.

33

11:12 p.m.

In the dream, I tried to tell my father something but the telephone kept interrupting. Each time I spoke, the thing rang.

Rinnggggg.

I struggled to open my eyes.

Rinnnggg. Part of the dream was real . . . I reached for the phone on the bed stand.

"Hello?"

"Darcy . . . it's Manny. I almost hung up."

"What's up?"

"The DVD."

"What about it?"

"Darcy . . . what do you know about subliminal persuasion?"

"Subliminal persuasion? Manny, what are you talking about?"

"How soon can you be here?"

"You at home?"

"Yeah."

"How do I get there?"

It took fifteen minutes to drive to Rodriguez's condo near Detroit's New Center Area. I turned into the parking lot, barely avoiding a speeding sports car on the way out.

I found the address and pulled into an empty space. I pressed the button at the front door and waited. I hit the button again. Voices came from the next building and three people emerged laughing. Inside, a stereo blared an ancient Motown song.

I tried the knob; it turned easily. I pushed the door open and stepped inside, finding myself in a small dark foyer. The only light came from the hallway straight ahead.

"Manny?" I called. "Manny!"

I proceeded slowly into the narrow hallway and called once more. Manny kept his condo as orderly as his office, so my heart skipped when I noticed a chair tipped on its side.

In the sparse light, I saw another hallway to my left, on the far side of the living room. I approached it, and looked right. Light came from underneath a closed door at the end of the hall. I reached it, pushed the door and it creaked open.

Nothing could have prepared me for the scene: blood everywhere . . . red splotches and streaks on the white wall . . . Manny Rodriguez in a red-soaked circle on the beige carpet.

"Manny! My god!"

Rodriguez opened his eyes, staring blankly. Trying to move, his limbs jerked sporadically. I rushed to him, kneeling at his side. I lifted his head and rolled it to the left. Rodriguez coughed, and spit red on my blue parka.

"Manny, what happened?"

"The . . . DVD . . . they . . ." Every word a struggle. "They took it . . ."

"Who, Manny? Who did this to you?"

Manny was fading fast. His eyes closed, then opened. This time the stare was blank. I reached up, pulled a pillow from the bed and pushed it under his head. I grabbed the telephone on the desk and hit nine-one-one. I gave the address to the woman, and told her to rush an ambulance.

Then I found the bathroom—in time to throw up into the toilet.

34

Saturday, Oct. 16—12:10 a.m.

I followed the ambulance to Henry Ford Hospital, five minutes from Rodriguez's condo.

Rushing through the automatic glass doors, I found myself a few feet from the reception desk. The expression on the face of the chubby, middle-aged African American woman at the desk told me to stop there.

"I'm looking for Emanuel Rodriguez. He was just brought here by ambulance."

"Are you a relative?" The woman typed something on the computer in front of her.

"No. A friend."

"I have no record of an Emanuel Rodriguez. You say he just arrived?"

"Minutes ago."

"It'll take time to process him," the woman said. "Have a seat in the waiting room."

"You'll call me?"

"Check back in ten minutes."

I walked into a small, brightly lit waiting room overflowing with people. I picked up a *Newsweek* and found an empty chair next to an older woman. Niles VanBuhler's picture peered at me from the cover. The story inside featured VanBuhler's surprising success in the spring primaries.

I tried to read, but my mind wandered. What had Manny found? Who had beaten Manny and stolen the disc? Were Bacalla or Roland involved somehow?

"Pardon me."

I looked up to see a tall black man in the uniform of a Detroit patrolman.

"Are you the lady who found the man they just brought in?" the policeman asked. "The man who was assaulted?"

"Yes. How is he?"

"I wouldn't know, ma'am. But I need your name, address and telephone number so our detectives can reach you."

"Why isn't someone here, now?" Rodriguez's beating deserved more than the mechanical recording of names and phone numbers.

"Busy night. A detective will call you tomorrow. Now may I have your name?"

I gave the policeman the information, then decided to check on Manny. But the woman at the desk said his information still hadn't reached the computer.

I found a bank of telephones in the small snack room and decided to tell someone from the agency what was happening. My first call, to Matt Carter, found his answering machine.

Reluctantly, I called Sean Higgins. He answered on the sixth ring.

"Sean? It's Darcy James."

"Darcy? What's up?"

"It's Manny Rodriguez, Sean. He's in the hospital."

"Hospital?"

"He's been beaten. Badly. They just brought him to Henry Ford Emergency."

"How is he?"

"No word yet. I just thought . . . well, I thought someone from the agency ought to know."

"I'll be there in twenty minutes."

As I replaced the receiver, the woman at the reception desk motioned to me.

"Still nothing on the computer," she said. "But I called upstairs. Mr. Rodriguez is in intensive care. His condition is 'critical'."

"Can I see him?"

"Sorry. Not unless you're a member of the immediate family."

I thought fast. "His brother is on the way. He'll be here in twenty minutes."

* * *

"You're his brother." I caught Higgins by surprise as he walked through the automatic doors. "He's in intensive care."

"His brother? Who's going to believe that?"

"The receptionist seems pretty busy. I don't think she'll ask for identification."

"What floor's he on?"

"Four, but you need a pass." I led Higgins to the desk.

"This is Manny Rodriguez's brother."

The woman looked at Higgins for a moment, as I held my breath. She finally opened a drawer, withdrew a numbered visitors' badge and handed it to him.

"ICU's on four."

Higgins started for the elevators with me close behind.

35

I described the scene at Rodriguez's condo, and the trip to the hospital. As we reached the elevator, the doors on our left parted, and I followed Higgins inside.

"Where do you think you're going?"

"With you," I said. "Until someone stops me."

The doors closed and a moment later opened on the fourth floor, the hallway vacant. The numbers and arrows on the wall across from the elevator told us to go right for the Adult Intensive Care Unit.

"I still don't think this is a good idea . . . I mean your being here," Higgins whispered.

"The place is deserted. Who's going to see me?"

The answer came two seconds later.

"Your passes, please." We found ourselves confronted by a woman as tall as Higgins, and nearly his weight. Standing hands on hips, she reminded me of a WAC drill sergeant.

"You need a pass to be on this floor," the woman said, walking closer. Her tag read "Dahner, Head Nurse, Intensive Care."

"We're here to see Manny Rodriguez." Higgins held out the plastic pass. Dahner examined it briefly, returned it and looked at me.

"Where's yours?"

"I . . . I don't have a pass," I said. "I'm the one who found Mr. Rodriguez."

"Sorry. No pass, no visit. You'll have to leave."

"Can you at least tell me how he is?"

"The doctor just left. He's alive. Vital signs are stable. That's all I can tell you."

Not exactly Florence Nightingale. She turned to Higgins. "You can have ten minutes."

"Is he conscious?"

"No." The way Nurse Dahner said it, it sounded like it would be a long while, if ever, before Manny regained consciousness.

36

Higgins followed the nurse through two metal doors into the Intensive Care Unit. Here, rooms with glass walls provided visual access to the patients inside. Through the glass Higgins heard the whirring, beeping and hissing of machines that kept those patients on this side of an even thinner wall between life and death.

Nurse Dahner took a sudden left into a glass-walled room. Higgins followed; as he walked inside a shock hit him like a rushing lineman. Even a career witnessing concussions, compound fractures and worse on the football field hadn't prepared him for what he saw. Manny Rodriguez lay surrounded by metal IV-stands, each draped with a bottle dripping fluid. Tubes were everywhere: nose, arms, chest . . . running underneath the covers. His eyes had swollen shut, and a respirator had been inserted in his mouth.

Higgins stood riveted to the floor, staring at the inert form, hearing the beeping and whirring of the machines that kept Rodriguez alive.

He had seen enough: it was time to get the hell out of there.

"How is Manny?" I asked as Higgins stepped out of the elevator.

"Unconscious. I can't tell you any more than the nurse did."

We walked toward the lobby of the emergency room, echoes of our footsteps piercing the silence. I couldn't help thinking about Rodriguez and how much his positive attitude meant to the creative group—and to me.

"What do you figure his chances are?" I asked Higgins.

"I'm not a doctor."

We avoided stating the obvious: that the bruised and bleeding body we had seen tonight bore small resemblance to the man we knew, and its chances of regaining the spark of life we knew as Manny Rodriguez might well be just as small.

37

Now

The good news came just past five o'clock. Ken Cunningham telephoned to say AVC had named Adams & Benson agency of record for their entire business.

Winning the AVC account called for a celebration. Higgins rummaged through the pantry closet and came up with half a fifth of Johnny Walker Red. He poured an inch or so into two tall glasses, added ice and water and we took them out on the deck. I was anxious to hear details of the AVC presentation, but first I wanted to know if Ken Cunningham was still on our side.

"We didn't have much time to chat," Higgins said. "He was at the airport and his plane was ready to leave.

"He asked me to tell you he's behind us. But of course insisted again that we turn ourselves in."

We talked about how the additional AVC business might change our lives. Both of us would gain additional responsibilities and, presumably, increases in salary. That is, if we managed to solve our present dilemma.

Higgins nodded off first, having gone without sleep for twenty-four hours. He headed for bed just after seven.

I stayed awake mulling over our situation. I couldn't get Manny's last words out of my mind.

What do you know about subliminal persuasion?

What *did* I know? I had read a few articles about the subject, but never really delved into it. If it somehow lay at the heart of why people were being murdered over the Avion disc, I owed it to Manny and the other victims to find out. I decided to visit the Gaylord library the next morning.

38

Now
Tuesday, Oct. 19—9:24 a.m.

Gaylord's library is small by big city standards, but it wasn't books I was after. I needed access to the internet. I still doubted that subliminal messages could influence the subconscious, but Manny had found something on that DVD. Something important enough that someone had tried to kill him.

I tried to minimize the risk of being recognized by pulling my shoulder-length brown hair into a bun and donning a scarf. Sunglasses completed my feeble disguise and it seemed to work. No one looked twice as I strolled past the checkout desk and into the room housing about half a dozen computers.

A Google search of "subliminal persuasion" coughed up a collection of subliminal help tapes for sale. I also found reports on that famous movie theatre experiment.

The man's name was James Vicary, and back in late 1957 he used a device he invented to flash the words "eat popcorn" and "drink Coke" onto a movie screen in Fort Lee, New Jersey. The words appeared every five seconds for 1/3000 of a second, too fast to be recorded by the conscious mind. According to the theory, though, the subliminal suggestion passed into the subconscious. According to the article, Vicary claimed the theatre registered an 18% gain in the sales of soda, and a 57% increase in popcorn sales.

The news created a media blitz followed by an almost hysterical reaction from a public fearing they might be brain washed in other ways. But Vicary failed in subsequent attempts to duplicate the results and subliminal persuasion faded into the nation's subconscious.

I clicked through a few more pages when a couple of articles I had never seen before caught my eye. One from Time magazine featured a Russian scientist's experiments curing drug addicts with subliminal messages in the mid-eighties.

If drug addicts could be cured through subliminal persuasion, could they also be created?

Another entry reported the FBI considered using subliminal telephone messages to convince David Koresh's followers to turn on him during the Waco confrontation in the early nineties.

It got even more interesting. I found a title: *The CIA and Subliminal Research*. Calling up the entry, my eyes followed down to a paragraph reporting that an article "Operational Assessment of Subliminal Perception" had appeared in the CIA's classified journal, *Studies in Intelligence*. The date of the original article? Early 1958, right on the heels of Vicary's 1957 movie theatre experiment. A rundown of its contents showed the CIA's interest in subliminal persuasion and its efforts under a top-secret initiative code-named MKULTRA in the mid-to-late Fifties.

I drilled deeper, entering MKULTRA into the search box. Entries spoke of MKULTRA as a CIA run project authorized by CIA Director Allen Dulles who had been concerned about rumors of communists brainwashing POWs during the Korean War. MKULTRA used private and public institutions to conduct experiments on unwitting subjects. The experiments ran the gamut from ingesting them with illegal drugs to exposing the subjects to, you guessed it, subliminal messages.

It took the Freedom of Information Act to make these details public.

I found more entries, including the testimony of Stansfield Turner, CIA Director in the late seventies, before a Congressional Committee. Turner acknowledged the project, denounced it and said it would never happen again.

But an intriguing question remained: *Why were the CIA, the FBI and the Russians so fascinated with a phenomenon that supposedly didn't exist?*

39

Saturday, Oct. 16—Early Morning

Manny's condition affected me deeply. I crawled into bed around four a.m. and couldn't sleep, despite the fact our presentation to Cunningham, Higgins et al loomed just hours away at eleven forty-five. I kept thinking about Manny. I needed to know what the police were doing to track down the animals who assaulted him.

Around seven a.m. I started dialing the Precinct, but got the runaround so many times I felt like a carousel. As a last resort, I tried my ex-husband.

Ordinarily Garry Kaminski's name would come up right after Charles Manson's on a list of people I'd ask for a favor. But I was desperate. This time, I asked for him and found Garry to be his usual, open-minded self.

"What do you expect me to do?"

"There has to be something you can do, Garry. Manny Rodriguez was nearly beaten to death. And, you're handling the Vince Caponi and Darren Cato murders."

"That's different. Caponi got two nine millimeter hollow points through his skull. The ME Report says someone rigged Cato's suicide. The D.A. calls both of those situations murder. You're telling me this Rodriguez guy was beaten during a robbery. I work Homicide. Best I can do is talk to the cops assigned to the case. Find out where they're at."

"That's just it, damn it," I said. "They haven't done a thing. I gave some cop my name and address at the hospital. One of your guys is supposed to call this morning. Some investigation."

"Look, Darcy, I know you're frustrated. How do you think I feel? Caponi's widow isn't telling us anything, either."

Caponi's widow? *Why would he mention her?*

"What do you mean, she's not telling you anything? What do you expect her to tell you, Garry?"

Silence. Garry realized he'd said something he shouldn't, and no way would I let the subject drop.

"It's been days since the murder, Garry. Why are you still talking to Caponi's widow? You said it, damn it. Now tell me."

Garry lowered his voice. "I need you to promise you didn't hear it from me."

"You've got it."

"The night Caponi was killed, he sent out *two* packages."

"Two? How do you know?"

"The Federal Express guy. We checked his records. One package went to Darren Cato at Adams & Benson, the other to Caponi's house. His wife signed for it."

"So?"

"She denies having received it. Says her signature was forged."

"Was it?"

"No way. The lab verified her signature, all right. But what the hell can we do? Throw a helpless widow in jail because she denies receiving a package? The media would be all over us."

"Maybe I can help."

"How?"

"We have common ground. First, her husband edited commercials our agency produced. Second, I'm a woman. She might talk to me."

"It's worth a try."

By now the clock read eight-thirty. Just enough time to grab a shower before heading for the office.

40

9:24 a.m.

What in the world was that piece of paper doing on my office desk? The square bar napkin had been folded neatly in half, then in half again.

The message on the sheet of yellow paper underneath it read, "Hope you like the line." It was signed, "Manny." I recalled a story Manny Rodriguez had told me about the writer who dreamed up the famous "No Car Rides Like a Rembly" line. He was in a bar at the time and wrote it on a napkin.

Manny must have left the napkin before he went home last night, figuring he'd found the right theme line for the campaign. We had settled for "The little car that could," but I still hoped for something better.

I unfolded the napkin. The words were printed in black magic marker.

A little Ampere goes a long way.

Perfect. It emphasized the Ampere's strong points while giving the car a definite personality. We'd insert the line into the layouts for presentation this morning. It fit so well, I didn't know whether to laugh or cry. Rereading the line, I laughed out loud.

Then, picturing Manny in Intensive Care, I cried.

41

11:34 a.m.

My group and I filed into the eighth floor conference room to find Sean Higgins and Lyle Windemere waiting.

The aroma of coffee filled the air, emanating from a shiny metal urn on a table against the far wall. Beside it sat two trays of bagels and sandwiches, which Bob Roy and Matt Carter dove for.

Higgins didn't waste time. "Cunningham, Adams and Rathmore will be here at eleven-forty-five." He motioned to the far side of the conference table. "You can set up over there."

"How long do we have?" I asked.

"You'll only have Ken for about twenty minutes. He flew in this morning, and has a two o'clock to Dallas."

My heart sank. I counted on pulling Cunningham aside after the meeting to fill him in on the past two days. Now I'd have to wait until Monday.

As we finished our preparation at eleven-forty, I noticed moisture on my palms for the first time, a reminder of the hundreds of jobs at stake. I rubbed my hands together to dry them.

Cunningham, Adams and Rathmore entered at precisely eleven-forty-five. The three couldn't have been more different. Even on Saturday Ken Cunningham wore the uniform: dark blue pinstriped suit and a red and blue striped tie. Joe Adams dressed casually in golf shirt and chino slacks that hung on him like a potato sack. C. J. Rathmore wore a gray herringbone jacket, the collar of his white dress shirt open.

As the former head of the AVC account, it was Cunningham's show. Ebullient as usual, he greeted each person by name. Stunned to hear about Manny Rodriguez, he asked to be kept updated.

Adams tried to emulate Cunningham's easy manner, but failed miserably. Apparently he couldn't let his hair down without downing alcohol first. Rathmore remained aloof, content to let the other two mingle with the troops.

"Let's get to it," Cunningham said finally. He smiled at Higgins. "I know Sean wants to be in front of the TV by the one o'clock kickoff. Who's Michigan playing today?"

"Wisconsin." Sean smiled sheepishly. "In Madison."

Ken turned to me. "Got something good to show us, Darcy?"

"I think you'll be pleased." Hopefully sounding more confident than I felt, I started in.

"For the theme line, we searched for a choice of words that suggested a cute, fun-to-drive personality, while emphasizing Ampere's range,"

I held up a board with the line printed in large block letters and noticed a slight nod from Cunningham as I read aloud: "A little Ampere goes a long way."

I lifted a layout board from the ledge and turned it to face my audience. The graphic depicted an early "horseless carriage" and the new Ampere side-by-side. Beneath the vintage vehicle the headline read, *The Twentieth Century came in with a roar.* Under the Ampere: *The Twenty-first Century comes in with a hummm.*

"The copy focuses on silent operation, acceleration, and range."

I searched for an expression: a smile, a nod, anything that would tip their reaction.

Nothing.

I reached for the next layout. The graphic: a photograph of the Ampere. I read the headline. "*With a zero to sixty time under nine seconds, the new Ampere passes a lot of things, including gas stations.* The copy features Ampere's acceleration and range."

Cunningham smiled.

I breathed a sigh of relief.

"When it comes to recharging the Ampere," I said, "we have two ideas. Both emphasize the Ampere can be recharged overnight, right in the garage. Both show the car attached to the recharging unit.

"One of the headlines reads *Watts up.* The other, *What a re-volting development.*"

Higgins smiled. "Your humor's right on target, Darcy. I like the way your ads convey the fun of driving the Ampere."

"I agree," said Cunningham. He turned to Rathmore. "I like what we're seeing, don't you, C. J.?"

"Of course." Rathmore, a bean counter more at home with bottom lines than headlines, seemed to welcome the opportunity of simply seconding Cunningham's remark.

Adams had also been waiting for Cunningham's reaction. He nodded and leaned back in his chair.

"How about ecology?" Cunningham asked. "The Ampere doesn't burn fossil fuel."

"Got it covered, Ken." I held up the ad M. J. Curtis and Will Parkins created with the picture of earth from space and read the headline aloud: "Here's the biggest reason of all to drive our new Ampere."

Cunningham leaned forward. "How far have you taken that TV idea you described the other day?"

I pushed a button on the TV monitor. The screen sprang to life with computer animation and music we'd patched together in the past forty-eight hours. In the end, Ken Cunningham's expression said it all.

"I think you've done one hell of a job. Now let's present it to AVC's Board of Directors and bring home the whole damn account."

Cunningham spent a few minutes on instructions. He asked for a write up covering our marketing background so he and Higgins could present it to the AVC Board.

"You'll be at the presentation, too," he told me. "But I know these guys; worked with them for fifteen years. I'll do most of the talking.

"Besides," he smiled, "It's going to be fun presenting this campaign."

42

Despite the euphoria from management's reaction, our celebration proved short-lived. After a short respite that included devouring the remainder of the bagels, donuts and coffee, we went back to our offices and began fine-tuning for the Big One: Monday morning's presentation to AVC's Board of Directors.

I left the building well after seven and settled for a movable feast: a tour of the drive-through lane at a McDonald's on Jefferson Avenue.

It was dark as I approached my neighborhood, and despite my personal pep talks, a queasy feeling gripped my stomach that had nothing to do with fast food. Whoever attacked Manny Rodriguez tried to kill him, and the questions kept coming. The biggest one of all: Was I next?

It seemed foolish to take chances. I parked next to a schoolyard two blocks away and began walking.

Light from houses blended with the yellow street lamps to brighten the scene and lessen my fears. Still, ominous patches of darkness between houses could easily conceal an attacker. I found myself walking faster.

It felt warm for October, pleasant really. I pictured families inside those homes eating dinner or watching television, and childhood memories came flooding back. I wished I could take my father aside as I'd done in high school and unload my fears. But this time it was up to me.

Entering my house, I left the lights out and double-checked the locks on front, back and side doors.

I phoned the hospital for word on Manny Rodriguez. His condition remained "critical."

I sat on the floor in my living room, reclining against the couch, my back to the window. Light from outside spilled in from behind me, illuminating the opposite wall. I decided it would be a great place for my prized oil by Quang Ho.

The worries of the past few days had my head spinning. I grabbed my trusty Martin guitar from its stand by the couch and began strumming quietly through the opening bars of the Eagles' *Desperado*.

That's when I heard the car door close.

43

I put the Martin back on its stand and turned to the window.

A car stood in front of the house next door. I scrunched down, keeping my eyes just above the window ledge, and inched closer, my nose nearly touching the glass. A figure rounded the front of the car and walked toward my house, a large man wearing a jacket and carrying something, a flashlight maybe.

He walked up the driveway. Ducking below the window, I pressed myself against the wall, not daring to raise high enough to look outside. I heard footsteps getting louder, then halting. The intruder had stopped directly on the other side of a thin, fragile pane of glass.

A beam of light swept through the room. I held my breath, afraid he might hear. Heart pounding, I watched the light dance around the room. Then it went away, and footsteps sounded again along the drive, moving away, toward the rear of the house.

I lifted my head and peeked over the window ledge. The man stood in front of the garage, flashlight on. The light went out and his dark silhouette disappeared from my line of sight as he walked to the back of the house. I heard him try the knob at the rear door. Locked. My eyes barely above the windowsill, I watched him reappear again and come toward me, along the drive.

Roland.

He stopped fifteen feet from me and bent down, out of my sight line. I heard a scraping sound, then a thud from the basement. A chill ran through my body. Roland had pried open a window and was inside my home.

Objects crashed in the basement as I ran to the front door. Footsteps pounded on the stairs off the kitchen. My fingers were wet with perspiration as I turned the dead bolt, then the handle, swung the door open and rushed through, slamming it behind me.

Out on the street, I ran for the car I left at the school.

In minutes that seemed like hours, I reached it. Out of breath, heart pounding, but alone.

I stopped at the first pay phone and dialed nine-one-one. Within minutes a squad car appeared, and two police officers followed me home to find . . . nothing. Roland's car had vanished, and so had he. One of the officers found marks where Roland had pried open the basement window, and the incident went down as a burglary, as common in big cities as paved streets.

* * *

Later, in bed at a Holiday Inn on Harper Avenue, I decided to call on Sid Goldman the next day. Sid would have some helpful advice. That is, if I could convince him I hadn't gone crazy, and he had regained enough strength to help. It had been six weeks since the heart attack; would I find him back on his feet or flat on his back?

44

Sunday, Oct. 17—1:14 p.m.

I pulled into the driveway of Sid's sprawling red brick ranch home in the suburb of Bloomfield Hills, just north of Detroit.

Three suitcases rode with me, in the back seat. I had gone back to my house just long enough to pack and telephone Sid. I'd check into another motel this evening.

A note taped to the screen door told me to walk around the house, where I found Sid enjoying the warm Indian summer sun on his patio. I'd feared he'd be weak and pale. Instead, Sid looked fit and tanned, decked out in a navy blue golf shirt, khaki slacks and brown loafers.

He rose to greet me, setting a copy of *Advertising Age* on the table in front of him. He took my hand in both of his with a firm grip.

"Darcy. Wonderful to see you. Welcome back to the Motor City."

"Thanks, Sid. But there's obviously a mistake here. Someone else must have had that heart attack. You look great."

"No." Goldman laughed. "It was me alright. Kicked the hell out of me. Four weeks ago, you'd have found me in my skivvies.

"Sit down, sit down." I pulled a chair away from the table and sat across from Sid.

"Mavis is at her sister's; I'm playing host. Let me get you some iced tea. Or perhaps a scotch?"

"Nothing right now, thanks."

Sid settled back in his chair. "You said you wanted to talk. Anything to do with the Ampere?"

Sid's mention of the Ampere caught me off guard. My expression must have telegraphed the surprise.

"Oh, I know all about the Ampere business," he said. "After I read about AVC's decision to review agencies, I called Cunningham. He drove out to fill me in." Sid smiled. "Probably afraid I'd have another heart attack if he didn't."

"The campaign's going fine. But there's something else . . . something really strange, Sid."

"What do you mean?"

I told him, starting with Vince Caponi's death, Darren Cato's suicide/murder, and the arrival of the suspect DVD at the agency. I described how the disc had been stolen, then turned up in Bacalla's office. At the mention of the name, Sid's face wrinkled as if he'd bitten into a lemon.

"Bacalla," he said.

"You know him?"

"Yes, of course. He came to the agency just . . . just before my heart attack."

I waited for Sid to say more. When he didn't, I prompted him. "What about Bacalla, Sid?"

"Darcy, you have stumbled onto something far worse than you could imagine."

"Bacalla?"

"The son-of-a-bitch is the devil reincarnate."

As I listened, Sid described his first meeting with Robert Bacalla, a cocktail party at the Adams mansion on Lake Shore Drive.

"I sensed something cock-eyed from the start. Said he was from Young & Rubicam in New York. Talking with him five minutes, I could tell he knew nothing about advertising."

"Did you mention that to anyone?"

"Ken Cunningham. Immediately afterwards."

"And?"

Sid looked me in the eye for the first time since Bacalla's name had come up. "Cunningham told me to mind my own business. He said the VanBuhler campaign pointed a national spotlight on Adams & Benson, and I should be glad Bacalla was there."

"Did you? Mind your own business, I mean."

"Hell, no. Bacalla was supposed to be some hot-shot political wizard who helped pull off Richard Columbo's upset. You remember . . . the guy who came out of nowhere to be elected Governor of New York? First thing I did was call some friends who'd worked on the campaign. They'd never heard of the bastard."

"Then who is he?"

"That's what I wanted to know. Before I went back to Cunningham, I needed facts. I started checking into people Bacalla talked to. Outside the agency, I mean. Our telephone system keeps automatic records of calls going in and out by extension.

Marlene Checkle, in administrative services, keeps the records on file."

"She let you see them?"

"You'd be surprised the influence the title 'executive creative director' carries. Anyway, there were calls to Washington, New York ... places you'd expect. But there were also calls to Tijuana, Mexico. Frequent calls."

"Tijuana?"

"The drug capital of the Western Hemisphere since the early nineties. Eighty percent of the cocaine that hits our streets passes through Tijuana."

"But phone calls to Tijuana don't prove Bacalla is involved with drugs. Do you know who the calls were to?"

"I was working on that when ... it happened."

"What happened, Sid?"

Goldman's hand shook visibly. "Darcy, what I've told you so far, and what I'm about to say can go no further."

"If that's the way you want it, Sid."

"I made notes of my little investigation. Kept 'em in a folder in my desk."

"Yes?"

"A week or so later, the notes had vanished. Instead, the folder held two photographs of my granddaughter, Stephanie. In one, her head was cut out of the picture."

"Sid, that's terrible."

"Worse. The pictures were taken by them ... whoever *they* are. The message was clear: they could get to her anytime they wanted."

"You took the threat seriously."

"You could say that. My heart attack happened the next day.

"This was no idle threat, Darcy. Let me tell you a story. There was a town near Tijuana. The mayor of that village, a woman, had crusaded against Tijuana's drug cartel. One day, as she addressed an elementary school class, two men broke in and grabbed an eight-year-old boy from the classroom. They chopped off his head and threw it back into the room."

"My god."

"An eight year old boy. That's the kind of people we're dealing with. The next child that happens to could be my granddaughter."

I thought back to Bacalla pointing his index finger at my head. A threat that seemed empty suddenly became frighteningly real.

45

I described my brush with the hit-and-run driver in the parking lot and the intruder breaking into my house.

Then I told Sid about Manny Rodriguez; how he seemed to have found something on the DVD, had been badly beaten, and was now in Ford Hospital.

"I heard about Manny," Sid said. "Hell of a shame. The guy'd never hurt a fly."

"Manny said you're the one who brought him to Adams & Benson."

"Manny was in the Army; weapons expert. Pistol or rifle, he'd shoot the eye out of a chipmunk at fifty yards. Unfortunately, his was one of the first classifications to go when they downsized the military.

"Sorry for getting off track. You were talking about your suspicions."

I finished my story quickly: the disc stolen from Rodriguez, his mention of subliminal persuasion and the possibility of a second disc in the possession of Caponi's widow.

"Subliminal persuasion? Don't tell me you believe in that crock?" Sid obviously didn't, and while I was beginning to believe anything could be possible, my imagination had taken enough punishment lately.

When I remained quiet, Sid spoke again. "You said this woman . . . the widow . . . is supposed to have a copy of the DVD in question?"

"Yes. But what I can't figure out is: what connection could that Avion DVD have with the Ampere presentation?"

"Beats hell out of me. But that disc seems to be the lightning rod for everything. The shooting of Vince Caponi, the beating of Manny . . . who knows, maybe even Cato's phony suicide. He worked on that Avion commercial, after all."

"So you agree I should visit Caponi's widow and see if she'll give me the DVD?"

Sid didn't answer right away. It was obvious he wanted to bring Bacalla down, but becoming too involved would certainly risk his granddaughter's life.

"Yes," he said finally, "I think you should go. But not alone."

"What's Caponi's widow going to do, shoot me?"

"It's not her I'm worried about. Once you have that disc, you're fair game for the people who want it. And they've already killed twice."

"Who'd go with me?"

"Me, if I were up to it."

"Yes, but you're not."

"Then Matt Carter . . . you said he knew Caponi."

"He'd be perfect, but he's at the agency preparing the television portion of the campaign for tomorrow's presentation to the AVC Board."

"In that case, the logical candidate is Sean Higgins."

"He thinks I'm nuts."

"Let's see if a phone call changes his mind."

46

4:45 p.m.

The shiny black bullet of a car slid next to mine in Sid's driveway, and the gullwing door on the driver's side rose. Sean Higgins placed a hand on the top of the windshield and swung himself up and out. When he stood, the roof of the car came barely to his waist. He had taken care that his black turtleneck and slacks matched the color of the car perfectly.

The car appeared to be a production AVC Avatar, but the rumble of the engine told a different story. It was an Avatar AVX, the souped up version of the Avatar. It had to be the same one I'd driven around the Grattan track three months ago.

"Hi, Sid, you're looking great."

Goldman pointed to the car. "What the hell's this? You sign up for the Grand Prix?"

"No chance. I wish it *were* mine. It's a prototype. The body's stock Avatar, but what's under the hood is twice as mean. AVC calls it the Avatar AVX; they're going to introduce this beast on the racing circuit next year."

Sid ran an admiring hand over the front fender. "This is no stock paint job either." The vehicle's gleaming skin appeared to have depth beneath the mirror-like finish.

I meandered over to the car and leaned down into an interior that resembled the cockpit of an F-16 jet fighter. I recognized the curved black instrument panel that wrapped around driver and passenger, the dual black bucket seats, and the shift lever immediately at the driver's right hand that shot the Avatar AVX through six forward gears. Behind this very steering wheel, I had clocked an official two hundred twenty on the straightaway at Gratten.

"No doubt about it," Higgins was saying, "this is a real man's car."

"How did *you* get hold of this real man's car?" I asked.

If Higgins caught the sarcasm he didn't show it. "AVC sent it over for a photo shoot. I got the keys from John Read in the photographic department. He's nervous as hell that I have it."

Higgins reached into the cockpit and hit a button. The gull-wing door on the passenger side lifted. "C'mon, get in. Let's not keep the lovely Mrs. Caponi waiting."

I'd much rather have gotten behind the wheel, but I put my left leg inside the passenger side, and lowered myself into the leather seat, thankful I wore slacks.

* * *

"Got a call from your ex-husband," Higgins said as we drove north on I-94. "He wants to talk about Cato."

"You didn't kill him, did you?"

"Of course not."

"Then you have nothing to worry about."

"Just the same . . ." He let the sentence die off.

Higgins tried his best to act nonchalant, sliding the Avatar in and out of expressway traffic. He obviously had more car than he had dealt with before. The Avatar AVX sprang like a pouncing animal at the slightest touch of the accelerator. Higgins held the steering wheel so tightly the knuckles of both hands turned white. I couldn't help smiling.

He continued looking straight ahead as he spoke. "Sid thinks there's something to your story."

"That's the only reason you're here?"

"That's the main reason I'm here." Then he grinned, looking over at me. "That and the fact I don't have any other place to drive this beast."

47

5:49 p.m.

Light was disappearing as we found Gracie Caponi's brick ranch in St. Clair Shores, a suburb north of Detroit.

I knocked on the aluminum storm door and the wooden door on the other side of the glass opened. Vince Caponi's widow wore a Detroit Red Wings sweatshirt and jeans, an infant balanced on one hip. Gracie Caponi was a short woman with brown, shoulder-length hair. She pushed the storm door toward us.

"I'm Darcy James, Mrs. Caponi. This is Sean Higgins."

"Do I know you?"

"Darcy and I are with Adams & Benson advertising," Higgins said. "Your husband was working on a project for our account group."

"We're friends of Matt Carter," I said. "He . . . we, believe your husband sent you a DVD the night he was killed."

"I'm afraid I don't know any Matt Carter. Or anything about a DVD."

So Mrs. Caponi was going to play games. According to Matt, he had known Gracie and her husband well. Matt had attended Vince's funeral.

"Like I told the police, and those two men this afternoon, I never got involved in my husband's business. Rachel, cut that out." She struggled to hold the squirming infant.

I knew she was stonewalling, but perhaps if I could get her talking . . . "You mentioned two men, Mrs. Caponi."

"Said they were from Adams & Benson, just like you. Asked about a disc Vince was supposed to have had. One guy did the talking, the other stayed in the car."

"Can you describe the man, Mrs. Caponi?" I asked.

"Dark, black hair. Looked Spanish, or Mexican maybe. No accent, though. Nice dresser. Had one of those thin mustaches."

Bacalla. The description fit the man like a condom, but I found something curious about Gracie Caponi's tone. She seemed nervous, maybe too nervous. If we could get inside and question her a little further . . . I decided to try.

"May I use your bathroom, Mrs. Caponi?"

"Sure, I guess so." The door opened and we stepped into a small living room. "Through that doorway, on the left."

Walking down the narrow hallway, I noticed a doorway that led into a small den. The room held a playpen along with the standard couch, easy chair and a TV tuned into Hollywood Squares. On the far wall hung a dozen or more framed photographs. Perhaps they could shed some light on Vince Caponi.

Moving closer, I saw a mixture of family snapshots and pictures of Vince Caponi with business associates: Caponi and Cato in tuxedos standing next to EMMY Chairman Rod Burton at the award presentation; Caponi along with Chris and Dave Sarris at the Caddy Banquet, a local award ceremony; and Caponi and Gracie with Matt Carter and a date, seated in a restaurant booth. Their body language, arms intertwined, said they were close business associates, if not friends.

"The lavatory is down the hall."

I turned to find Gracie Caponi in the doorway, holding her daughter. Sean Higgins appeared behind her, palms outstretched in a "Sorry, I couldn't stop her" posture.

"Mrs. Caponi, you said you didn't know Matt Carter. But this picture . . . obviously you knew Matt well."

"I think you'd better leave."

"Mrs. Caponi . . . Gracie," I said. "Matt and your husband were friends. We want to help."

Gracie's expression softened, so I went on. "Federal Express records show that your husband sent a copy of that disc to you. One of our friends almost died trying to keep another copy from getting into the wrong hands. We want to make sure the right people see it."

Gracie Caponi began to cry. She set her daughter in the playpen and wiped her eyes with the sleeve of her sweatshirt.

"I didn't . . . didn't know what to do. Vince called me that night to say he was FedExing a package here. He said to hide it . . . not to show it to anyone."

"Where is it?" I asked.

"C'mon."

She led us through a small kitchen to a side door and into a brick garage in back of the house.

"Here. Take it." Gracie seemed relieved.

"You're doing the right thing," I said.

"I told the cops I didn't have it. What will they do?"

"Sergeant Kaminski is an old friend," I said. "I think he'll understand."

Higgins and I said good-bye and started walking.

"Darcy?"

I looked back. Standing alone under the garage's single light bulb, Gracie Caponi appeared small and fragile. "What could be in that package that someone would kill Vince over?"

"I don't know, Gracie," I said. "But I promise we'll find out."

48

7:15 p.m.

Street lamps cut yellow streaks through the darkness as Higgins and I walked down Gracie Caponi's wet driveway. The aroma of freshly-watered grass hung in the air.

Higgins backed the Avatar out of the driveway and we started down the street, Higgins still babying the car. A few blocks from the house he turned to say something and noticed my expression. "What is it?"

"A car . . . following us."

"You sure?" He searched the rear view mirror.

"Don't you see it? A Dodge Viper."

"Yeah . . . there. You sure it's following us?"

"Turn here and see."

Higgins cut the wheel sharply at the next street, nearly running onto a lawn. The Viper followed. Higgins pressed tentatively on the accelerator pedal and the Avatar responded with a quick jump from twenty-five to thirty-five miles per hour.

The Viper saw the ten and raised five, creeping closer.

"Turn again."

Higgins feathered the brake pedal, and guided the Avatar cautiously into the turn.

"Still there." I could have saved my breath; Higgins' eyes were fixed on the rear view mirror. He pressed the accelerator again, coaxing the AVX to forty miles an hour.

Higgins turned my way. "What do they want?"

"The DVD. What do you think they want?"

Higgins inched the accelerator toward the floor, tacking on another ten miles an hour.

As the Viper drove under a street lamp, I saw two men inside, one talking into a cell phone.

"I can't go faster on these side roads," Higgins said. "Let's get to a main street." He cut sharply at the next intersection. The bright lights of Gratiot Avenue lay dead ahead, the Viper followed close behind.

49

The traffic signal at Gratiot came up fast and red. Higgins swung the Avatar around the corner without stopping, and eased into traffic. A horn blared behind us. Sprinting the same corner, the Viper had cut someone off.

With Higgins coddling the Avatar like a delicate work of art, we'd never lose the Viper. Our attention suddenly focused on three flashing blue lights behind us, a police car coming fast. The Avatar's digital speedometer read sixty miles per hour. In the Avatar AVX, it felt like thirty-five. The police car weaved its way through the maze of vehicles behind us. The flashing lights passed the Viper. I never thought I'd be glad to see a traffic cop, and I bet Higgins felt the same way. Guiding the Avatar AVX over two lanes, he pulled into the parking lot of a small strip mall.

The policeman leaped from his car and ran toward us. "Everybody out. Hands against the car. You inside," he yelled at me, "that means you."

The cop continued shouting. Higgins leaned against the AVX, placing one hand on the extended gullwing door, the other on the roof. The policeman patted him down.

"Okay, Miss, you too." The cop pushed me against the vehicle. I put my hands on the car as he gingerly patted me down.

"Officer, we were being chased."

"You're driving a stolen vehicle."

"Stolen?" Higgins took his hands off the Avatar and stood facing the policeman.

The cop's hand was on his holster as he turned to Higgins. "Got the registration?"

"It's an experimental vehicle, a prototype, owned by American Vehicle Corporation . . . loaned to Adams & Benson, the advertising agency. I'm a vice president."

"It's reported stolen," the cop replied.

"Stolen? That's crazy."

The Viper pulled into the small parking area. As driver and passenger emerged from the vehicle, I recognized Bacalla and Roland.

"Bacalla," shouted Higgins. "Tell this man who we are."

"Never mind that," said the policeman, turning to the two, "who are you?"

"Bob Bacalla and J.R. Roland," Bacalla said. "We're with Adams & Benson, AVC's advertising agency. We spotted this Avatar AVX a few miles back, and we've been following. It's an experimental model, very valuable."

"Let's see some I.D."

Both men produced driver's licenses. Bacalla reached into the Viper and retrieved an attaché case. He produced several documents with Adams & Benson letterheads, enough to convince the policeman.

"You know these two?" he asked, motioning to Higgins and me.

"I've seen them around the Adams & Benson building."

"Are they authorized to drive this vehicle?"

"As I said, it's very valuable. I can't answer that. You'd have to ask someone on the AVC advertising account."

"I run the AVC account, you ass," Higgins roared. "Tell him who I am."

"Get away from the car," the cop shouted. Roland was on the driver's side of the AVX, leaning across to the glove compartment. He straightened up, holding the Avion DVD.

"Just getting this DVD," Roland said. "It's agency property." I noticed he slurred his words. There were sirens in the distance, more cops on the way.

"It's also evidence," the policeman said. "It stays with the car."

Bacalla started toward the patrolman. "Officer, that DVD is needed in a high-level conference tomorrow morning."

While the policeman concentrated on Bacalla, I saw Roland pocket the disc, and pull another from his coat.

"Sean," I called, "Roland switched DVDs. The submaster's in his pocket."

As Higgins started for Roland, the cop stepped in his way. Higgins avoided him, but Roland suddenly had a pistol in his hand.

Higgins surprised me. I hadn't figured him for the hero type; it must have been a reflex instinctive to an athlete. He took a step toward Roland, grabbed the big man's gun hand and pushed it away from his body.

A flash of light followed and a "pop" as the gun fired so close I caught the acrid smell of cordite in my nostrils. The policeman dropped to one knee, clutching his right side. Drawing his own gun, he pointed it unsteadily at Roland.

Higgins still held Roland's gun hand. He shook it violently, and the weapon hit the ground. As they struggled, Higgins appeared overmatched at first. Roland equaled Higgins' height, but was stockier and had moves straight from a Jackie Chan film. But Roland seemed slow. Higgins said later he'd caught the aroma of alcohol on the man's breath. The fight ended with Higgins wrestling Roland to the ground and tearing the DVD from his coat pocket.

Bacalla, meanwhile, had drawn his own gun and was yelling at the policeman, trying to convince him the shooting hadn't been Roland's fault.

Realizing Bacalla would soon have that gun pointed at us, I jumped into the driver's seat of the Avatar AVX and waved for Higgins to follow. He hesitated, then leaped into the passenger seat.

"What the hell are you doing?"

"Driving," I shouted back, hitting the button that lowered the gullwing doors. "You'd better buckle up."

A twist of my wrist sparked the engine to life. I slammed the gearshift lever forward and wheels spit gravel. Second gear came a split second later at sixty-five. In the mirror, I saw the cop slump to the pavement, and two figures run for the Viper.

Flashing lights in the distance grew larger.

50

Monday, Oct. 18—2:23 a.m.

Dad. I know you're sleeping and I'm actually glad I'm speaking to your voice mail right now. What I have to say isn't easy, and I don't have answers for a lot of the questions you're going to have. If you haven't heard already, you're going to, about a policeman being killed. They think Sean Higgins and I . . . had something to do with it. We did. I mean, we were there. But it was an accident. Sean Higgins wasn't even holding the gun. The police are looking for us and we have to hide for a while. I know we can prove we're innocent . . . but I can't go into that right now. I hope to see you soon. Good-bye, Dad. I love you.

51

Now . . . or Never
Wednesday, Oct. 20—1:23 p.m.

My visit to the Gaylord library had confirmed my suspicion that the Avion DVD contained some sort of subliminal message.

Fortunately, for once Higgins agreed.

We sat on the deck, a warm breeze blowing through the trees nearby, mulling over the consequences of what I had just learned.

"We need evidence," Higgins said. "That DVD; we've got to examine it like Rodriguez, and presumably Caponi, did: frame by frame. If you're right, we'll find some sort of message."

A blue heron flew by out over the lake, barely ten feet off the water. I turned back to Higgins. "We need the right equipment."

"There's a television station in Traverse City that would have the technology. If we go near it, though, it could be the last TV station we visit for thirty years."

We sat in silence for a moment.

"Sean, shouldn't there be copies of that commercial in Detroit? At the TV stations that ran it?"

"Yeah."

"Let's ask Matt Carter to visit Channel Four, find their copy and run it on their equipment."

"Good idea; but I wonder how he's handling the fact that we're wanted by the police."

"Let's get him on the phone and ask."

52

Carter's voice mail message reported he was on a video shoot. A call to his cell phone ended in another recorded message.

"There's nothing we can do until we talk to Carter," I said. "Let's take a walk and give our minds a rest."

The sky was clear, temperature in the high sixties with a warm breeze drifting out of the west. I wore shorts and a sweatshirt, Higgins jeans and tee shirt with a red windbreaker. We talked as we strolled along a sandy trail just wide enough for two hikers. Higgins recognized each specie of tree, and called them out by name: oak, northern white pine, poplar, cedar, birch. Small white and brown birds darted from branch to branch, punctuating their flights with high-pitched peeps. Rounding a corner, we surprised a black squirrel, sending him scurrying up a pitch-stained pine.

The bright sun and pleasant surroundings helped push the crisis into the background. I found Sean easy to talk to, almost charming, away from the agency.

"Look, up there." I pointed to a clearing in the trees ahead. Blue water appeared through the branches as we got closer.

"Hart Lake," Higgins said. "Uncle Frank and I came here bluegill fishing twenty years ago. Those were some of the best times of my life."

We stood quietly for a while, looking out over the water. Hart Lake was small and round, no more than a half mile across. Only two boarded-up cottages, one white the other blue, broke up the array of green, orange, red and yellow foliage. The bright sun, coming from almost directly overhead, made the blue water sparkle with silver.

I caught Sean's profile in the corner of my eye, and inhaled a hint of his cologne. I was beginning to experience a closeness to this man I hadn't felt since my early days with Garry. I fought an urge to lean against him; afraid he'd move away.

Then I felt him brush against my arm. On purpose?

We stood like that awhile, enjoying the beauty of the vista and the feeling of being close. A breeze wafted by, carrying the pleasant aroma of dry autumn leaves. We were in the eye of a hurricane: calm here, but violent winds were swirling somewhere out there; winds neither of us could control.

It seemed too soon that Sean spoke. "Ready to go back?"

"Sure."

The spell broken, we headed back along the trail.

It was a beginning.

53

8:36 p.m.

I got through to Carter later that evening, sitting on the living room couch, portable phone to my ear. As we talked I gazed out the front window, squinting into the darkness at a growing ball of light on the beach where Higgins nursed a bonfire.

"What the hell's going on, Darcy? Cops are all over the place looking for you and Higgins."

"It was an accident, believe me." I gave Carter a quick synopsis of the events.

"I knew it, Darcy. Higgins may be a jerk, but he'd never kill anyone. Not that policeman, not Darren Cato. Cops are calling Cato's death murder, but I'm sure it wasn't Higgins."

"Glad you feel that way, Matt. We need your help, desperately."

"What can I do?"

I ran through my theory and Carter agreed to visit Channel Four the next day. He had spent a summer there as a college student several years ago, and still knew many staff members.

"Can you be there first thing in the morning?"

"I've got to spend time on the Ampere commercial with Klein. Cunningham's called for a progress report by three. Promising the Ampere spot on air next Monday might have gotten the account, but it's put a hell of a burden on us."

My pause telegraphed the disappointment I felt. Carter picked it up.

"Darcy, I'll have the Avion commercial on the monitor at Channel Four as soon as I can after that. I'll call you by four o'clock."

54

I picked my way through the darkness, following light from Sean's fire, now a roaring blaze on the beach.

Standing by the fire, I related my conversation with Carter: his reaction to my explanation of the shooting and the plan to visit Channel Four tomorrow. The news called for a toast and Higgins ran up to the cottage for two glasses of wine.

Sitting on a log close to the flames, I heard waves lapping at the shore behind me. I welcomed the warmth. Despite the unseasonably mild temperatures of the day, the October night was downright cold. The crackling fire shot sparks upwards, into a sky so peppered with stars they seemed to meld together in spots, forming glowing white masses. The screen door slammed, and I saw Higgins' silhouette against the cottage lights, making his way with two glasses of wine.

We clinked glasses, and I felt the pleasant warmth of the wine blend with the heat of the fire. Why couldn't we be two people on vacation, enjoying the moment? I wished our problems would disappear.

"I hate this waiting," I said. "Sitting up here seems like we're in limbo."

"What would you suggest? Riding back to Detroit on a white horse and putting the bad guys in the hoosecow?"

"Not hoose*cow* . . . *gow*. Hoose*gow*. If you'd watched old cowboy movies on TV with your dad like I did, you'd know all about hoosegows."

"I never knew my father that well. He never seemed to have time for me. At least until I was all-state in football.

"It was my mom who insisted I go to Catholic school. She would give my butt a good whipping when I complained a nun had paddled me for screwing up."

"What was it like? I mean, being a football star."

"Okay, I guess. Football saved my parents a lot of money . . . got me through college on a full ride."

"That was it? Saving your parents money?"

Higgins looked at his glass. "You know the most important thing I ever got from football?"

"Tell me."

"My father's attention." He spoke slowly, on a journey into unfamiliar territory. "It's the old story: the father who's married to his job; too busy for his wife and kid. Other dads came to Little League games. Mine was at the office. Uncle Frank was more of a father. I couldn't wait for summers, when I'd come up here."

I'd never seen this side of Higgins. He exhibited a tenderness, a vulnerability, miles from the hard-driving advertising agency vice president I thought I knew.

"Football changed that?"

"It did when I made all-state. My father suddenly realized he had a son. But it was almost too late."

"Too late?"

"He died the summer between my freshman and sophomore years at Michigan."

"I'm sorry."

I waited for Higgins to speak, but when he sat looking into the fire, I changed the subject. "Tell me something: what was it like running out of that tunnel in front of a hundred thousand screaming idiots in Michigan Stadium?"

It did the trick. Higgins turned back to me, a grin sliding across his face. "Trying to get a rise from me, calling U of M fans 'idiots,' huh? I'll tell you one thing: it was a hell of a thrill. You can't believe how juiced you'd get."

"Must have been a kick being Big Man on Campus?"

"Sure. Everybody wanted to be your best friend. But it's a two-edged sword."

"How do you mean?"

Higgins fell silent again. For a moment I thought he hadn't heard my question.

"When I was a kid," he said finally, "we used to play a game. I'm going to tell you a secret I've never told anyone."

"I'm listening." Did it concern Darren Cato?

"But in return, you have to tell me something you've never told anyone."

"How will you know I'm not making it up?"

"I'll believe you."

"Okay. You first."

"When I was at U of M, my girl friend . . . the one I dated in high school, went to Michigan State. I loved her, and thought she loved me too."

"She didn't?"

"I found out she dated a guy who played halfback for State. We broke up between our sophomore and junior years.

"That fall we played State at home. I was a linebacker then . . . before they switched me to fullback."

"We were up by four with ten seconds to go. This guy, her boyfriend, had been trash-talking me all afternoon, and it was my last chance to give him a shot. They were on our fourteen, and their quarterback dropped back to pass. Our defensive coordinator had called a blitz, and I got by the first blocker. All I could think about was that jackass . . . how he probably slept with my girl . . . the girl I loved.

"Anyway he was blocking for the quarterback, who had dropped back farther than he should. I had a clear shot, but I only saw that damn halfback. I hit him with everything I had . . . drove his butt into the ground."

"Must have been satisfying."

"Yeah. But it would have been a hell of a lot more satisfying if the quarterback hadn't lobbed a pass into the end zone for six."

"The coaches were mad?"

"Mad? The coaches were always mad when we lost. But on the game films it looked like I made an error in judgment. Not one person, no one . . . until you . . . has ever known we lost the game because I went after the wrong guy on purpose."

"What about the girl? Did you see her again?"

"I wasn't exactly best man at their wedding," Higgins shook his head and smiled. "Now it's your turn."

I thought for a moment. "I know some women do it sooner, but I was about eighteen."

"Yeah?"

"Well, some friends of my parents, the Moores, were in Europe on a business trip. Their son Mark stayed with us. One night, when my parents were out at a party . . ."

"Yeah?"

"Mark came up to my room."

"Yeah? Yeah?"

"He had some pot . . . some marijuana."

"Uh-huh. Go on."

"We smoked it."

"And then . . ."

"That was it. We smoked pot."

"That's it? That's all?"

"Well, we opened the windows, of course. The place absolutely reeked from the smoke."

"Your deep, dark secret is that you smoked pot when you were eighteen?"

"That's right."

"I tell you about blowing a football game that cost us a trip to the Rose Bowl . . . and you tell me you smoked pot?"

"Hey, I was weak," I said, trying not to laugh out loud. "What can I tell you?" Just when I thought Higgins would explode, he started to chuckle. It turned into a funny, high-pitched sound that seemed entirely out of character for a man his size. Hearing him, I broke out too.

My hysterics got Higgins laughing harder. With tears rolling down his cheeks, holding his sides, he fell backwards off the log he had been sitting on. I tried to stop his fall, and rolled with him.

We stopped laughing, and for a moment we laid looking at each other, our faces glowing in the firelight. Then Higgins leaned closer, and I closed my eyes.

We kissed. It was tentative at first, but developed into a warm, lingering embrace that neither of us wanted to end. Our tongues met, and I felt a dizziness that had nothing to do with the wine.

"I'm sorry," Higgins said. "I've wanted to do that for a long time."

"I didn't exactly fight you off."

"If we ever get out of this mess, I hope we can spend some time together. Go to dinner, a football game . . ."

"We're going to have a lot of time the next few days. And funny as it sounds, Sean . . . if I had to be in this disaster with anyone, I'm glad it's you."

Our lips met again. The kiss was longer this time, the warmth of it making me forget the coolness of the air.

"I . . . I think we'd better get to bed. I . . . I mean to sleep," Sean stammered as we parted. I could almost see him blushing in the darkness.

Sean found the small shovel he had used to dig the fire pit, and threw sand on the coals. I picked up the two empty glasses and headed for the cottage.

Tomorrow was another day.

55

6:26 p.m.

Carter had promised to call by four with his findings at the television station, but the hour came and went. It was well past six when the phone finally rang.

"Darcy, Matt."

"Yes, Matt; what did you find on the DVD?"

"There is no DVD. Channel Four doesn't have 'Avion on the Beach.'"

"What?"

"I checked Channel Seven, too. Same story."

"What about the other stations?"

"The people who work in their video libraries have all gone home by now. I'll call tomorrow. But I've got a feeling I'll hear the same answer."

"What happened? Where are the DVDs, Matt?"

"They were recalled. By the agency."

"Recalled? DVDs don't get recalled. Stations are forever bitching because they have to store them."

"Yeah, well these DVDs were. And get this: who do you think recalled them?"

"Curt Neumann," I said. "He's media for AVC, isn't he?"

"That would have been my guess. But it wasn't. It was Andi Hall."

"Andi Hall? Who the hell is Andi Hall?"

"She's new. She's the media buyer for the VanBuhler team."

I broke the news to Higgins. Standing beside the kitchen table, he ticked off his assessment of our situation.

"No DVDs at the stations. No way to find out what's on the DVD we have. And the cops wanting to arrest me for murder. Can it get worse?"

I shrugged my shoulders. It couldn't, I hoped.

But the next morning I'd learn how wrong I was.

56

Thursday, Oct. 21—9:01 a.m.

"You're front page news again," Matt Carter announced. "Not only is Higgins a suspect in Cato's murder, now they're saying he shot Vince Caponi."

"What?" I nearly dropped the telephone.

"Police ballistics say the gun Higgins dropped after the cop was shot is the same one that killed Vince Caponi."

"Sean didn't kill Cato. I'm sure of it. And he didn't drop that gun. Roland did."

"Unfortunately the cops think otherwise."

"What about fingerprints?"

"The only prints on the gun are Higgins'. Roland wore gloves."

"Higgins grabbed the gun during the struggle."

"You don't have to convince me. It shows you've been right all along. Roland shot Caponi and I'm sure he killed Cato, too. Those guys play for keeps."

"Are the police still hanging around?"

"Kaminski practically lives here. Between the cops and all the talk about Monday night's party, it's damn hard getting any work done."

"What's that about Monday night?"

"The agency's throwing a party for the Jets-Forty Niners football game. Sort of a thank you to us grunts for our part in winning the AVC business. The game will be on two giant TV screens in the lobby. They're setting up bleachers, hot dog stands, the works. And of course, the Ampere commercial debuts at half time."

"Is it ready?"

"Jimmy Klein says it will be. Oh, and I almost forgot: more good news."

"Lay it on me. Good news I can use."

"It seems Channel Two still has a copy of 'Avion on the Beach.' They neglected to send it back to the agency."

"Can you get it?"

"The station manager, Ed Blake, is taking it home after work. He lives about a mile from my apartment."

"How will you check it out?"

"He's got some high-priced equipment in his basement. I'll call you from his place."

57

8:55 p.m.

Carter finally called—much later than we expected.

"Bad news, Darcy. Real bad."

"Matt? What's going on?"

"Ed Blake's dead."

"Blake? Dead? What happened?"

Carter had gone to Blake's house before seven. He heard a car running in the garage, opened the door and found the garage filled with carbon monoxide fumes. He dragged Blake from the car and tried artificial respiration. A nine-one-one call brought an emergency unit. Too late.

"What are the police saying?"

"Suicide."

"What do you think?"

"I think it's another murder dressed to look like suicide. When I talked to Blake this morning, he was fine."

"What about the DVD?"

"It was on the front seat."

"When are you going to look at it?"

"I just did. I'm in the Media Center. I ran it frame by frame."

"And?"

"Nothing, Darcy. Sorry."

"Whoever killed Blake took the real DVD and replaced it with a harmless one."

"That's what I figured. But where do we go from here?"

"Look, Matt. We can't get to you, but you can come here. We have the DVD Gracie Caponi gave us. Come get it, check it out for us."

"Tell me how to get there and I'm on my way."

* * *

With Gaylord a three-and-a-half hour drive from Detroit, I didn't expect to hear from Matt much before twelve-thirty. It surprised me when the phone rang closer to ten-thirty.

It wasn't a good surprise.

"Darcy, I can't get there."

"What's the problem?"

"The cops are tailing me. They must have followed me from Blake's earlier, but I didn't see them until about half an hour ago."

"Where are you?"

"A restaurant in Saginaw. They're outside. I've tried to lose them but can't. I don't want to lead them to you."

"Go on home. We'll think of something."

"Sorry, Darcy. But I've got to be honest: I'm kinda glad the cops are here; or maybe I'd be dead, too."

58

10:58 p.m.

I sat slumped on the living room couch, Higgins in a chair next to me. Carter's news had taken a toll on both of us.

Higgins set his magazine down and headed for the television.

"Let's see if we're still headline material."

"I'm going to bed. Every time our faces are on TV, there's a better chance someone like your friend Mrs. Gordon will recognize us."

"Don't worry about her. Old Mrs. Gordon's in a world of her own."

I started for the bedroom, but the news program's fast-paced opening caught my attention. I watched the screen fill with a succession of reporters on location, then dissolve to a studio set. Two talking heads, a man and woman, looked eager to dive into the disasters du jour. The thin, serious-looking young man took the lead story: the latest polls showed Niles VanBuhler pulling into a dead heat with President Nordstrum.

The second story, read by the blonde anchor, a Diane Sawyer look-alike, centered on the armed robbery of a bowling alley lounge in Gladwin.

"Looks like we're old news in Northern Michigan at least." I started to get up from the couch, but the next story stopped me in my tracks.

"The search for the sports car cop killers is widening, according to Roseville, Michigan police," the male anchor read. "Sean Higgins and Darcy James are wanted for questioning in two murders: a video editor killed last week, and an advertising agency producer originally thought to have committed suicide. But yesterday's report placing the pair in the Traverse City area appears to be a false alarm."

The scene shifted to a young woman standing next to a black sports car. She reported the vehicle turned out to be a Bugatti, not the notorious AVC Avatar.

The newscast returned to the studio. "Weren't you at the University of Michigan around the same time as Sean Higgins?" the Diane Sawyer look-alike asked the male anchor.

"Yeah, and that's why I don't get it," said the man. "I didn't know Higgins personally. But besides being a top athlete, he had a reputation as a good student and, well . . . a gentleman."

"He's got me pegged, alright." Higgins smiled. "Model student."

"Frankly," the male news anchor continued, "I can't believe he killed anyone. There must be more to the story."

"And we'll have more . . . more news that is . . . right after this . . ." Diane almost-Sawyer said as the station broke for a commercial.

Higgins hit the off switch. "Well, someone's on our side."

I was suddenly wide-awake. "Maybe that's the answer."

"What answer? What do you mean?"

"That guy on the news might be our last hope to see what's on the Avion DVD. What's his name?"

"Phil . . . Phil something."

"Phil Speilman. Let's call him."

"Now?"

"Right after the news."

59

A recorded voice at WTVC answered with a list of department choices. Higgins pressed "five."

"Speilman."

"Mr. Speilman . . . this is Sean Higgins."

"Sean Higgins? Sure you are. And I'm Bo Schembechler."

"Speilman . . . I'm taking a huge chance calling you."

"Then why are you?"

"Because you're my last hope proving my innocence in those killings."

"And how can I do that?" From his sarcastic tone it seemed clear Speilman didn't believe it was Higgins.

"Speilman, you said you went to U. of M. the same time I did. Ask me a question."

"A question?"

"Something about football. Didn't you go to the games?"

"Never missed."

"Then ask me something."

"Okay. The Iowa game our senior year . . . what was the final score?"

"Twenty-seven, twenty-four. We pulled it out in the last minute."

"The winning touchdown . . . who scored it?"

"Bobby Campbell."

"Anyone could know that."

"Speilman, listen: J. D. Huffer faked to me, then handed off to Campbell. He went over Irv Rabideau's block to score."

"You're right. I had forgotten the details."

Higgins let out his breath. "If I pass, let's get on with it. I need your help."

"You've got it. That is . . . if you're really innocent."

"I swear it. I'll explain when I see you. And guarantee you an exclusive. Right now, here's what I need . . ."

Higgins told Speilman about the DVD.

"We've got what you need. Just get me the disc."

"I can't let it out of my sight, so it has to be at night. With no one else there. Can you run the equipment?"

"Of course. You don't think us news types are just pretty faces, do you?"

"We need to do this right away."

"How about tomorrow night? The studio clears out after the news. Park in the back lot. You'll have to punch in a code to get in. It's three, four, seven, five."

Higgins scribbled the numbers on a pad next to the phone.

"See you tomorrow at midnight."

60

Friday, Oct. 22–Late evening

Higgins left for Traverse City after a late supper.

It occurred to him that the meeting could easily be a trap. Snaring a wanted fugitive would be great publicity for Speilman and the station. Still, the meeting represented their last hope.

Thinner than he appeared on television, Speilman stood almost as tall as Higgins. After a short greeting, the two walked down a narrow corridor and through a steel door into one of the station's small editing suites.

"Best equipment between Detroit and Chicago," Speilman said, motioning toward a bank of monitors, recorders and assorted editing devices.

Speilman sat at the controls, facing three video monitors; Higgins took the seat next to him.

"What are we looking for?" Speilman asked.

"This whole mystery started with an editor who found something on this DVD. The commercial has a bunch of bikini-clad women standing around an Avion on a beach. I want to view it the way he might have."

"How's that?"

"First, with all those babes bouncing around in bikinis, let's assume he wasn't viewing the commercial for a good look at the vehicle."

"You're saying the headlights that turned him on weren't on the car?"

"Exactly."

"Let's try it." Speilman pushed a button on the console and the monitor lit up with the scene of the Avion racing along the sand. As the car slowed to a halt, the bikini-clad women ran to it. Speilman froze the frame on three faces: a blonde and two brunettes.

"You're on the right track. Let's keep going . . . this time in slow motion."

Speilman pushed a button and the picture began to move slowly and the scene changed, focusing on another girl, a stunning blonde. Speilman touched a button and the screen froze. "This more like it?"

"Hold on. Did you see anything? Words? Just before this?"

"Let's see." Speilman pushed a button and the scene reversed, frame-by-frame, until . . .

Both men stared dumbly at the monitor. Speilman had frozen the frame to stop the action completely, but it took both a minute to realize what they saw.

There it was, just as Darcy predicted. Suddenly Higgins understood why Vince Caponi, Darren Cato and Ed Blake had been murdered. Why the people who killed them wouldn't rest until Manny Rodriguez died . . . and why those same people would most certainly be coming after them.

The two men stared at the screen for a long moment.

Then Higgins reached for the phone on the control panel in front of them.

61

The clock on the living room wall told me the eleven o'clock newscast had been over more than an hour. By now Higgins could have examined that DVD fifty times.

Why hadn't he called?

I walked to the kitchen, lit a burner and started to boil some water for tea. Feeling a draft, I noticed the window over the sink open a crack. As I leaned forward to shut it, I sensed movement outside. Someone, something lurked just outside the cabin.

I switched off the overhead kitchen light and peered out into the darkness. Nothing. I turned the light back on.

A knock at the front door startled me.

I switched on the porch light. Peeking through one of three small diamond-shaped glass windows, I saw a middle-aged man bundled in a red and black-checkered hunter's jacket. I wondered if the storm door was locked. I hoped so.

As I pulled the wooden door open, I saw the visitor clearly through the storm door. A stocky man with dark hair and a thick, black mustache completely covering the space between his nose and upper lip, he smiled as he nodded a greeting.

"Hello, Miss . . ."

"Yes?"

"Hope it's not a bother. Saw your lights on, and my mother . . . Mrs. Gordon next door? She's having one of her migraines. I wonder if I could trouble you for some aspirin."

He seemed friendly enough, and I hated the thought of the frail Mrs. Gordon suffering a migraine. I fussed with the latch on the storm door, and finally pushed it open.

"Thanks." The man rubbed his hands together as he entered the cottage. "Sure cools off fast once the sun goes down. I'm Tom Gordon." He offered his hand.

"Mary . . . Mary Johnson." I found the hand icy cold. If the man recognized me from the television news reports or newspapers, he didn't show it. Regardless, I didn't want to chance giving my real name.

"I'll see if I can find some aspirin." I headed for the bathroom, but the sound of the telephone brought me to a halt.

"You were expecting a call this late?" Gordon asked.

"It's . . . it's probably my friend. He's in Traverse City."

I could have answered the phone in the kitchen alcove, but instead walked to the back bedroom, out of Gordon's earshot, and lifted the receiver.

"Hello?"

"Darcy, Sean."

"Sean, where . . . what's happening?"

"You were right about the DVD."

"What did you find?"

"The stakes are much higher than we ever imagined. Darcy, listen to this: digital discs record action at a rate of thirty frames every second. This disc, the Avion submaster, carries a message every twenty-ninth frame. The message appears so quickly, the conscious mind never sees it. But it gets implanted big time in the subconscious."

"What message?"

"Two words: VanBuhler and leadership."

"My god, they're trying to corrupt the election. No wonder VanBuhler is coming on so fast. We've the evidence we need, Sean. Now we've got to get it to the right people."

"We'll leave tomorrow. But for now, I don't want you there alone. With what we know, it's not safe."

"Sean, be serious. Where else can I go?"

"Until I get back, I want you to go over to Mrs. Gordon's."

"That old lady? You think she's going to protect me?"

"I don't want you in that cottage alone. These people, whoever they are, always seem to be a step ahead."

"Not this time, Sean. Mrs. Gordon's son is here. I'm perfectly safe."

"Who?"

"Mrs. Gordon's son. He's here with me. He came to get aspirin for his mother."

When Higgins spoke, the words slid down my spine like a sliver of ice, leaving me chilled to the core.

"Darcy, Mrs. Gordon doesn't have a son; or a daughter. She and her husband were childless."

62

I heard a sound and turned to see the intruder standing in the doorway. The urge to run nearly overwhelmed me, but I kept my composure and continued talking in an imaginary conversation.

"I'll pass along the message, Jack." I replaced the receiver. It would take an hour for Higgins to get here. I couldn't let this man guess I was on to him.

"Bad news?" he asked.

"Why would you say that?"

"Your face. You look surprised, even scared."

"I'll get your aspirin." I brushed by the man and walked to the bathroom, opening the medicine cabinet. I held out the bottle.

"Take it."

The man took the aspirin and started for the door. He got as far as the kitchen alcove when he turned. "Jack? You called your friend Jack."

"That's right. That's his name . . . Jack."

"Not Sean?"

"I think it's time for you to leave." My legs suddenly felt like rubber bands. I leaned backward against the stove for support, almost scorching my hand on the burner heating the pot of water.

"I've got a better idea," The man's tone changed, no longer the friendly, apologetic neighbor. "I'm going to stick around and see who your friend *really* is."

He reached behind his back and closed the door.

"What are you going to do?" I fought to keep my voice from shaking. My palms felt sweaty.

"I just want to talk to you both. Relax."

It was a lie, of course. With stakes as high as a Presidential election, no way could we be left alive.

The intruder stood in front of me, motioning toward the living room. Leaning against the stove, I felt the handle of the pot on the burner. The water should be boiling. My hand shook as I made a half-turn to the right and grabbed the pot handle. Spinning back to my left I hurled the contents directly into the man's face.

"Ahhhhhhh . . . !" A horrible, high-pitched scream erupted from the man's throat as he grabbed his face with both hands. I bolted past, jerked open the front door, pounded the handle of the storm door and ran into the cold night air. I tore around the cottage, heading for the back, dodging trees, my feet fighting for traction against sandy soil. I raced across the lighted clearing behind the cottage and into the dark forest. Ferns whipped against my jeans as I dashed through the darkness.

"Bitch! I'll kill you!" The voice wailed somewhere behind me. I hoped the scalding water had blinded him. I stopped to look back, lungs burning. Hiding in the trees, I crouched sixty feet behind the cabin. The light over the back door shone brightly.

Just as I began breathing easier, the man bolted around the corner of the building, stopping in the center of the spotlighted area. Even from this distance I could see he suffered immense pain. He rocked back and forth, making some sort of noise, moaning. He reached inside a coat pocket and withdrew something. As light spread in front of his feet, I realized it was a flashlight.

The man stood stock still, cocking his head one way, then the other. Listening . . . listening . . . straining to hear the slightest crackle of leaves underfoot, the sound of a twig snapping. Hearing nothing, he began walking toward the stand of trees.

Toward me.

The flashlight's beam came closer. I snatched a look behind me. The dirt trail leading to the road lay fifty more feet away. I doubted anyone resided in the cottages along that road; the buildings had been boarded up when Higgins and I arrived.

The man walked faster now, his light extending past the first few trees. I eased backwards, toward the dirt road.

CRACK!

Betrayed by a footstep. The dry twig snapping seemed like the report of a rifle shot. I froze. To the left stood a huge pine. I took a single giant step and slid behind it.

The sound hadn't escaped my pursuer. He pointed his flashlight toward my position and began walking. The light danced through the pines, coming dangerously close to where I huddled behind the tree. Pine needles crackled under his feet, the sound growing louder. He now moved to within inches of me, on the opposite side of the tall pine. His footsteps stopped and his breath rasped as he sucked in the night air. I pinned my arms against my body, locking my elbows under my rib cage. My heart pounded with such force it hurt. The light played around the trees, stopping here, there . . . as the man tried desperately to find me.

I fought to keep my breathing under control; terrified the man might hear me. The moment seemed frozen in time. Then the footsteps began again, this time moving past. I inched around the tree, keeping the trunk between me and the source of crackling leaves and snapping twigs. The man moved to the rear of the lot, circled back and traced the property line toward the front of the cottage. I let out a breath as I watched the flashlight disappear around a corner.

I suddenly became aware of another sensation: cold. The night was painfully frigid. Racing from the cottage, I hadn't worn a coat or sweater, and the cold bit through my jeans and thin cotton blouse.

To my left I made out the shape of the small tool shed behind Mrs. Gordon's house. Was it possible a sweater or jacket hung inside? I crept toward the shed, gingerly at first, grimacing as my footsteps caused crackling sounds against dry leaves and pine needles. As the cold became overbearing, my steps came faster. I kept my arms folded in front of me, my hands rubbing them in an attempt to keep warm.

The shed couldn't have been more than six feet square. Inside, I saw nothing but darkness. Crouching low, I crawled in, reaching back to close the door. My purser was out there, and could be coming back.

Wrapped in darkness, I found myself shivering violently. I quickly but carefully felt along the wall behind me.

Nothing.

Feeling backwards, now along the floor, I felt . . . a sweater. I tugged, but it was caught. Remembering the matches in my jeans pocket, I retrieved the pack and struck one.

As the sudden flash of brightness died and my eyes became accustomed to the dim light, I saw to my horror what the sweater had caught on.

The cord around poor Mrs. Gordon's neck and an agonized expression on her old wrinkled face told a horrific story: death had come with a great deal of pain.

63

Higgins guided the blue Lumina onto Peninsula Drive. Driving as fast as the narrow road allowed, he found a grassy area just off the sandy trail where he killed the headlights and engine.

Still a half-mile from his uncle's cabin, he climbed out, eased the car door closed and began walking quickly. As his eyes adjusted to the darkness, the sandy road appeared as a light gray strip, with the trees on either side black silhouettes. He half walked, half ran on the edge of the road, ready to duck for cover if headlights appeared.

He'd had time to think in the hour since leaving Traverse City, and a lot to think about. He feared for Darcy's safety, and dreaded what he might find at the cabin.

He had weighed the significance of what he discovered. Darcy's guess had struck the bull's eye. Bacalla and his people were using Adams & Benson, its facilities and employees, to carry out an outrageous act of deceit on the American people.

And to do that, they had chosen the commercials of the AVC account, *his* account.

Higgins wondered how many were involved, how many of the people he knew and talked to every day? The thought that he worked side by side with people involved in this conspiracy made him sick.

He'd stopped twice along the way from Traverse City and called the cottage from pay phones without success. He tried to force speculation to the back of his mind; reality would come soon enough.

Higgins continued along Peninsula Trail as it wound to the right. Close to the cottage now, he moved slower. Mrs. Gordon's cabin came first, on the left, and as he stared through the trees, he caught a glimpse of light.

Strange to see light coming from Mrs. Gordon's place this late, but he continued on. Uncle Frank's cabin was next. Higgins stole past the sandy driveway, spotting lights in the kitchen and living room. Another sixty feet and he left the road, slipping through the trees toward the lake. Reaching the beach, he turned into his uncle's front yard and crept along the water's edge. Hidden in the darkness, he had a clear view. The living room was brightly lit, and empty. He cocked his head, listening. The only sound came from the lake behind him, its waves rippling softly into the shore.

Crouching low, he inched closer to the cottage, vaguely aware of sweat beads forming on his forehead and upper lip. The inner, wooden door stood wide open. He walked quietly to the storm door and tried the handle, pulling it open.

"Darcy?"

Nothing. He listened for sounds from the back bedrooms. Silence.

Moving slowly, he nearly tripped over a pan upside down on the floor. Stooping to pick it up, he noticed wet carpet surrounding it.

"Mr. Higgins, I presume."

Higgins jumped, startled by the sound. Looking up, the sight shocked him more: a man of medium height in a red and black hunting jacket, pointing a pistol at his chest. The man's face was as red as the shirt, and horribly distended. One eye was swollen shut, the other open and wild looking.

"Your girl friend did this," the man hissed. "Boiling water."

"Where is she?"

"Screw you. You know too much already."

"Enough to put you away for a hell of a long time."

"Let me guess. You found the message in that Avion DVD. Too bad you won't get a chance to tell anyone." The man raised the pistol.

There was movement in the darkness of the bedroom behind the gunman. Darcy? It had to be.

"Someone already knows," Higgins said. "A TV reporter in Traverse City. Anything happens to me, he'll tell the cops what he saw."

The man lowered the pistol. "So you didn't leave the DVD with him. You have it."

"How can you be sure?"

"If the reporter had the DVD, he wouldn't have to *tell* what he saw. He would *show* them."

The pistol came up again. "You've told me all I need to know."

64

I entered the rear door of the cottage moments after the man who had been chasing me.

I heard voices from the living area, and peering out from the darkness, I saw Sean with the man in the black and red jacket. The man had his back toward me, but the conversation made it clear he held a gun.

So did I; a loaded single-shot .22 rifle I found in Mrs. Gordon's shed.

One shot. One chance.

Would I have the nerve to shoot? Did I have to? If I just pointed the rifle, could I convince him to drop his gun?

Or, would he shoot me instead?

I stepped into the living room, rifle at my shoulder. The man in red and black couldn't see me, but Sean's eyes went hubcap wide as he spoke. "When the reporter calls the cops they'll investigate."

The man raised his gun. "They'll find diddly. By then your DVD will be at the bottom of that lake out there."

Sean screamed. "Good god, Darcy. Shoot."

One shot. One chance.

The man whirled toward me and uncertainty vanished with the squeeze of the trigger.

The report of the rifle was magnified inside the cottage, the air smothered by the smell of cordite. The man fell to the floor.

I dropped the rifle. "I didn't want to kill him."

"If you hadn't pulled the trigger, I'd be lying there."

Sean's eyes went from the body on the floor back to me. "Where'd you get the rifle?"

"The shed next door." I suddenly remembered: "Mrs. Gordon. He killed her. She's there in the shed."

I looked at the man on the floor. "What do we do about him? And how about poor Mrs. Gordon?"

"We call the police now, they'll be on our tail. We'll have to hide him in the shed.

"Then we pack, lock up and get out of here."

The body on the floor sent a shiver through me as I was struck by the realization that I had killed another human being. I felt guilty. But strangely, the guilt didn't spring from the shooting. It came from the fact I didn't feel a bit guilty that I killed him.

Does that make sense?

65

Saturday, Oct. 23—2:06 a.m.

The headlights of the Chevy Lumina pointed the way south on I-75, Higgins at the wheel. As we rode, the conversation centered on what Higgins found at the studio: the frames with "VanBuhler" and "leadership" repeated throughout the commercial. We both agreed there had to be more AVC commercials; probably with VanBuhler's name matched with words like "diplomacy" and "economic savvy."

"Those are the qualities pollsters ask people to rate candidates on," I said. "No wonder the man's off the charts."

Sean's eyes were nearly closed.

"Sean, let's find a place to stop."

We took the next exit and found a motel not far from the expressway. I donned the same "disguise" I'd used at the Gaylord library, pulling my hair back, wrapping it in a scarf and applying eye makeup darker than usual.

I needn't have bothered. The night clerk, a young man about eighteen, was half-asleep. After I filled out a card and paid in cash, he handed me a key.

"Two-eighteen. Around back, second floor."

The room contained one king-size bed. Too tired to argue over propriety, we climbed under the covers and fell asleep.

* * *

On the expressway by noon, we drove south past towns with names like West Branch, Rose City and Pinconning. Sean seemed wide-awake after eight hours of sleep.

I kept thinking about the shooting the night before and picturing the stranger in the checkered jacket lying lifeless as we placed him in the shed next to Mrs. Gorden. Trust me: no matter who's at the other end of the bullet and how justified the shooting may have been, it's not easy getting over killing someone.

As we drove, the stress of the shooting was slowly replaced by the satisfaction of finally having the evidence to prove the existence of a conspiracy, a conspiracy to overthrow the Executive Branch of the United States Government.

Once the plot behind the murders and phony suicides came out, our innocence would be obvious.

During the next day or so we'd contact the police and FBI. Of course we couldn't just ride up to police headquarters. We needed a plan and thankfully, I had awakened with one. We'd have to wait for dark, but it included the perfect place to hide; the one place absolutely no one would ever think of looking for us.

66

Saturday 6:34 p.m.

"What the hell are you doing here?"

My ex-husband stood in the doorway of his apartment wearing a white tee shirt, blue jeans and an astonished expression.

"Don't make us stand in the hall." I breezed past him, looking over my shoulder to see Garry move aside to let Sean enter behind me.

"You two are crazy." Garry checked out the hallway before closing the door.

"If we aren't, we will be by the time this thing's over," I said. "Garry, this is Sean Higgins."

"I've seen his picture."

Neither offered his hand. It was obvious Sean felt uneasy meeting my ex-husband.

"Aren't you going to invite us to sit down?" I didn't wait, plopping down on the brown leather sofa against the wall. Given the evidence we had, I admit I felt a bit cocky.

From the couch, I saw most of downtown Detroit through the picture window. The room itself: genuine Garry. Besides the sofa, the only furniture was a recliner chair and an entertainment center with its large-screen television. I guessed the total contents of his refrigerator were probably a partial six-pack of beer and leftovers from his last pizza.

"Do you understand how much trouble you're in? Every police officer in town is looking for you, and more than a few would just as soon have you dead as alive."

"Garry," I said, "we can not only prove our innocence, but have evidence that next week's Presidential election has been compromised."

"What the hell are you talking about?"

"That DVD with the Avion commercial on it. Caponi and Cato were killed over it."

Garry looked at Sean. "The jury's still out on Cato. What about the DVD?"

"We found out why Caponi and Cato were murdered, and why Manny Rodriguez was beaten."

Sean jumped in. "There's a subliminal message on the DVD."

"A what?"

"Every twenty-ninth frame of the commercial contains a printed message. VanBuhler's name and the word 'leadership.'"

"This is the same DVD I watched in your conference room? I didn't see any subliminal message. Just broads in bikinis and a car on the beach."

"That's the point," I said. "With the words appearing every twenty-ninth frame, the human eye doesn't see it, at least consciously. It registers in the subconscious."

"It's registering like pure BS to me."

"The CIA and FBI have conducted studies on the effects of subliminal projection for years, Garry. It's very real to them."

"What did you say the message was? Something about VanBuhler and leadership?"

"The election's days away," I said. "Someone's making sure Niles VanBuhler gets elected. If we're going to stop them, we have precious little time."

My ex-husband listened as Sean and I took turns explaining the events of the past week. We covered the confrontations with Bacalla at Adams & Benson, the chase that ended with the shooting of the policeman and, finally, the killings at Lake Manuka.

"And who do you think is behind all this?" The note of skepticism in Garry's voice rang like a bad chord.

Till now, I hadn't told anyone about the conversation on Sid Goldman's patio, or about his granddaughter's picture. But it was going to take all the ammunition we had to convince Garry, so I told the story, complete with details.

"I gotta be honest with you," Garry said, "if it wasn't you telling me this story, Darcy, I'd run you both downtown right now."

"Garry, the DVD we're talking about is down in the car," I said. "We have proof."

"Proof? That's no proof. Anyone in your business could make that disc. You could have done it to create an alibi."

"Garry, somebody's trying to mess with the government of this country, and you . . ."

"Darcy, it doesn't matter what I believe. Besides everything else that's gone on, you two are accused of killing a cop. There are people with a hell of a lot of power putting on pressure to find you at any cost."

"The election's an eye blink away. What *will* convince you?"

"It's not me you have to convince."

"What about Robert Bacalla?" Sean asked. "Have you checked him out?"

Garry grimaced. Sean had struck a nerve.

"Well?" I asked.

"Bacalla's in Washington."

"Washington?" I couldn't believe it. "He's a murder suspect. What the hell's he doing in Washington?"

"He *was* a suspect. But after you two split, VanBuhler's people started applying pressure to get the judge to set bail. The fact that you two disappeared helped their case immensely. We held both of them . . . Bacalla and Roland. We checked records, prints, everything. Nothing suspicious on either. Roland was even decorated in the Gulf War."

"If they're out on bail, isn't there a limit on how far they can go?" asked Sean.

"Technically, yes."

"Technically? What do you mean, technically?" Now I was shouting.

"VanBuhler's people again. Rumors say this time it came from the top. Both men got orders back to Washington."

"And you didn't stop them?"

"No one downtown asks my opinion. The Chief and I aren't exactly drinking buddies."

"So now, you're going to arrest us?" Sean said it more like a challenge than a question.

"You think I've got another choice, lay it on me."

"Help us check out Bacalla and Roland," I said. "I'm sure they not only committed multiple murders, including two phony suicides, but they're deeply involved in the conspiracy."

"I'll consider it," Garry said. "Meanwhile, as long as you're here, you'd better eat something.

"There's beer and part of a pizza in the fridge."

67

Garry couldn't remember exactly when he had ordered the pizza, a fact painfully obvious when he lifted the lid of the flat cardboard box.

"I think you've created some new life forms here, Kaminski," Sean said.

"Penicillin. With all the venereal disease out there, a single guy can't be too careful."

Sean nodded and surprised me by smiling.

"I'll leave the penicillin to you Romeos," I said. I pointed to the telephone number on the pizza box. "Me, I'm ordering a new pizza. Cheese, pepperoni and mushrooms . . . and hold the mold."

Waiting for the pizza, I had an idea. Using Garry's computer to access the national telephone directory, I found the number of Margi Wallace, a woman I knew at the New York office of Young & Rubicam, one of the agencies Bacalla claimed to work for prior to Adams & Benson. Luckily, Margi was spending this Saturday night at home with her boyfriend.

"Yeah, I remember Bob," Margi said after we exchanged greetings. "Great guy, always good for a laugh. Too bad about the accident."

"Accident?"

"You didn't know? Bob died in a car accident."

"When's the funeral?"

"Funeral? What are you talking about? Bob Bacalla died three years ago."

The pizza arrived as I finished the conversation with Margi Wallace, and we huddled around Garry's kitchen table.

"If Bob Bacalla bought the farm three years ago, who's at Adams & Benson?" Garry was a master of the rhetorical question.

"You took his fingerprints," I said. "They didn't tell you anything?"

"Like I said, Roland was easy. A war hero, for god's sake. But Bacalla? There was no record of the guy's prints anywhere."

"Any other way of tracking him?" Sean asked. "I mean finding out who this guy really is?"

"Might be. It's a long shot, though."

"What is it?" I asked.

"When we take fingerprints, we also do mug shots."

"Yeah?"

"Well, there's sort of a computerized mug shot book. You scan the suspect's photo into the computer, and it's compared with photographs of known criminals. All over the world, if you need it."

"Can you do it?" Sean asked.

"Yeah."

"Tonight?" I asked.

"Tonight?" Garry checked his watch. "It's ten minutes to ten."

"It's also ten minutes to police headquarters," I said. "And less than two weeks to the election."

Garry shrugged. "Let me finish this pizza."

* * *

I followed Garry to the door. "Thanks for putting up with Sean. He may not be the most diplomatic person in the world, but he's really very sweet."

"You two got something going?"

"Is it that obvious?"

"Nah, call it a cop's intuition."

"Yeah, I know. Good luck. There's a lot riding on what you find."

68

I began to worry.

Garry had been gone an hour on an errand that should have taken thirty minutes at most.

Sean and I passed the time watching a cable news report of the campaign. The polls showed the President regaining a narrow lead over VanBuhler, with the Democratic challenger still a distant third. The report was sprinkled with sound bites of the three candidates addressing crowds in Chicago, Muncie and Indianapolis. VanBuhler had a ready smile to go with his glib comments and made-for-the-camera good looks.

The media adored him, but I wondered what they'd say if they knew the truth.

As the report from the campaign trail ended, I found myself watching the clock. What could be taking Garry so long?

"I'm going down to the car to get our clothes," I said.

"I'll go, too. I don't think it's smart for you to go alone."

"We're more likely to be recognized together."

"Then I'll go."

"You're too easy to spot. I can put my hair up in a scarf, and pull it over my face.

"See?"

"Okay," Sean said, "but if you're not back in five minutes, I'm coming after you."

"I'll be quick. You hear me knocking, let me in. I don't want to stand out in the hall."

69

Higgins stood behind the door as Darcy left, to avoid being seen from the hallway. Once she was gone, he returned to the sofa and the news.

Minutes passed when he heard hard, fast knocking. Darcy was either awfully fast, or had forgotten something. The knocking came again as he approached the door. Again standing behind the door, he grabbed the handle and pulled it toward him. A feminine shape breezed past.

"Lord almighty! I thought you were going to make me stand out there all night in this," she said as she flew by.

Only after Higgins closed the door did he realize it wasn't Darcy. The woman had her back to him, and her hair was long and blonde, not brunette. She wore a bright red lingerie outfit straight from one of those sexy catalogs. And while he hadn't yet seen her face, he could definitely see her cheeks. If this was Victoria, she wasn't hiding any secret.

"Surpri..." the woman began to shout, whirling around, arms in the air. Against all laws of physics, she seemed to halt in mid-air, her jaw dropping open as she saw Higgins.

"Who the hell are you?" The woman landed in a crouch, folding her arms in front of her in an attempt to shield her ample breasts.

She needed bigger arms.

"I... I'm Sean Higgins. Who the hell are you?"

The woman started to answer, but another knock cut her short.

70

Standing in the hallway, it seemed forever before Sean opened the door. I ran in, a suitcase in each hand.

"I made it all the way without . . ." I stopped dead, dropping the suitcases on the floor. Sean stood next to a nearly naked and very buxom blonde. "What the hell's going on here?"

"Maybe I should be asking you two what you're doing in my fiancé's apartment."

"Fiancé?" Garry hadn't mentioned being engaged. I looked at the half-naked woman, then at Sean, his face nearly the same red hue as the woman's negligee.

"Hey, I know you," the woman said, looking at me, then Sean. "I saw your pictures on TV, and heard Garry talk about you."

"I'm afraid you're right," I said. "Garry and I were married at one time." *Looks like he's gotten over it, though.*

"You two don't look like criminals to me."

"We're not," I said. "That shooting was a terrible mistake."

The woman stuck out her hand. "In that case, I'm Rose Dombroski. Call me Rosie D. Everybody does."

"Glad to meet you Rosie D, I'm Darcy James."

Rosie turned to Sean, offered her hand, and caught him staring at her barely covered bosom.

"Oh . . ." he said, coming out of the trance, "I'm Sean Higgins." *The jerk.*

"Guess I'd better put something on. I was planning on surprising Garry. Guess the surprise was on me."

The phone on the entertainment center rang. Rosie reached for it.

"Yeah?" There was a pause as she listened.

"Yeah, they're here now." Another pause. "Yes, Garry, I introduced myself. In fact, you could say they've seen a lot of me."

"He wants to talk to you." Rosie gave me the phone.

I took it. "What did you find?"

"Something I'm not sure I believe."

"Try me."

"Reason I didn't get back right away: I tried the computer for photographic matches in the U.S. first."

"Yes?"

"I got back three possibilities, two already in federal prisons. The third's been dead for three months."

"Go on."

"Then I tried the international file. Covers the whole world."

"And?"

"If I'm right . . ." he hesitated. "God, if I'm right . . ."

"What is it, Garry?"

"What do you know about international terrorists?"

"Too much nowadays. And most of them seem insane."

"Ever hear of a guy named Mendoza?"

"No. Should I have?"

"Ernesto Mendoza. A.K.A. 'Mendoza the Monster.' A South American terrorist. No one really knows for sure exactly who he is. In fact, he may not exist."

"You found a mug shot of someone who doesn't exist? What the hell are you talking about?"

"No one knows much about him. The man we think is Mendoza was born in Colombia. Went to school in Bogotá, then disappeared for ten years or so. Turned up in Europe, where he supposedly knocked off people... big people... for big money. Government officials, that sort of thing. He eventually went back to South America."

"And you think Bacalla is this guy Mendoza?"

"I'm not sure. But Darcy, if Bacalla is Mendoza, you've got to stay away from him. Leave him to the police."

"What do you mean?"

"You're talking about an animal who's coldly murdered people on three continents for no other reason than money. Sometimes for no reason at all. The file says Mendoza's first killing happened when he was only fourteen. Know how? He showed off a stolen pistol by pointing it at a passing car and killing the driver. Just like that."

"My god."

"The case never went to trial. The only witness was murdered walking out of a police station."

"If there's doubt that Mendoza exists, how did his picture wind up in the computer?"

"Good question. What we have is a computer-enhanced photo of a face in the crowd. It was taken just before the assassination of a Latin American presidential candidate."

"And it looks like Bacalla?"

"Not exactly, but a hell of a resemblance. The picture's nearly five years old. These guys are known for altering their appearances with plastic surgery."

"Can you have him arrested?"

"No. But I'm going to call the D.C. police, right now. The judge allowed Bacalla to leave Detroit under the condition that he agreed to check in with the Washington police. They supposedly have him under surveillance. But I want to make damn sure they keep a tight watch on him. Tell Rosie I'll be home in twenty minutes."

I was going over the conversation with Garry with Sean and Rosie when the phone rang again. Rosie answered, listened for a minute and then put the receiver back on the wall.

"It was Garry," she said.

"What did he want?" I asked.

"He said he called Washington . . . to make sure the cops were watching your guy Bacalla?"

"Yes?"

"Washington cops say he's been missing since Thursday. They think he might be headed this way."

71

11:36 p.m.

Matt Carter joined us in Garry's apartment and sat cross-legged on the floor in front of the couch.

My phone call had found him in bed after a dozen hours at the agency putting finishing touches on the Ampere spot. The urgency in my voice snapped him awake. He knocked on the door twenty minutes later.

A few feet from Matt, Rosie D rode the arm of Garry's recliner. She had replaced the negligee with a tight-fitting blue t-shirt and jeans.

As the conversation progressed, I surveyed this gathering, the white and yellow lights of Motown playing outside the window, and realized more than just my future depended on these few people.

My hopes had taken an uppercut to the chin. Garry's attitude had changed since he discovered the so-called Mexican Connection.

"These are drug people, terrorists. It's time to stop playing cop and let the people downtown handle it."

"What are the odds they'll believe us?" Sean asked.

Garry shifted uneasily in his chair. "I'll be behind you all the way."

"That's not what Sean asked." My eyes bored into my former husband. "A plot to compromise the U.S. Presidential election would be hard to swallow even if the Attorney General discovered it. What are the chances of authorities believing a couple of fugitives?"

"I can't answer that. But I *am* saying that you can't mess with these people. They knew you were here, they'd kill all of us without a thought."

"Garry, you're the only hope of stopping them."

Garry didn't answer immediately. "Understand where I'm coming from," he said finally. "Twelve years on the force . . . and I'm hiding two fugitives. One of the guys from my precinct stops by for a beer, sees you two, and I'll be lucky to get a job as a crossing guard."

"You're saying you're going to turn us in."

"You're catching on."

"Look, Garry. You've let Bacalla and Roland go. The least you can do is give us more time. I've got a couple of ideas, but we need two or three days."

"You've got twenty-four hours."

* * *

"What are those bright ideas you mentioned?" Sean asked, yawning.

Sean, Carter and I remained in Garry's living room. Garry had retired for the night, Rosie D had gone back to her apartment after inviting me to sleep in her extra bedroom. Sean would ride out the night on Garry's couch.

"Damned if I know. But if I hadn't said something, we'd be headed for jail. So let's think fast."

We spent fifteen minutes pouring over options. In the end, we had only one: find evidence. The A & B Media Center was the place to start, and Carter was the man.

"Look for anything suspicious," I told him. "The commercials had to be doctored there. VanBuhler's people have used the Media Center for months."

"You've got it. Tomorrow's Sunday. The place'll be deserted. I'll be there early."

72

Sunday, Oct. 24—9:58 a.m.

"They must have you guys humping. This is the second Sunday in a row you've been here." The young dark-haired security guard pushed the logbook forward and handed Matt Carter a pen.

"They can't run the place without me, Scotty."

The mammoth A & B lobby stood empty and probably, Carter suspected, so did the rest of the building. He walked to the elevator and pushed the button for seven. He'd have plenty of time to search the Media Center. He wished he could be equally confident of what to search for. "Evidence," Darcy had said. But what the hell was that?

On seven he headed for the Media Center. He walked through the waiting room, down the narrow hall to the editing suite. Switching on the light, he stopped dead in his tracks.

Just inside the door sat a large plastic mailroom cart on wheels, packed with flat cardboard envelopes. The kind used to ship DVDs.

Picking one from the cart, he saw a label addressed to a Minneapolis television station. He cut the tape with his thumbnail, extracted the disc and read the label: "AVC Ampere: sixty second commercial."

The copies had been made on Media Center equipment. Given the secrecy surrounding the Ampere, they would remain here until after the vehicle's introduction tomorrow night.

Carter inspected the disc, wondering if it were infected with a subliminal message. With the election hairbreadth close, it made sense that the conspirators would make a final attempt at influencing voters.

Carter began pushing buttons on the control panel. He inserted the DVD and, as the commercial began, pulled one of the levers forward, slowing the action until the spot ran frame by frame. There was the Ampere in one city, followed by another. Singers appeared on screen, then the action returned to the car. Carter ran the entire commercial, finding nothing.

He reached for another DVD, this one addressed to the ABC-TV affiliate in St. Louis, and soon had it running frame by frame. Color bars, then Ampere driving city to city. Suddenly the words "VanBuhler: Leadership" appeared on screen, then vanished. Carter reversed the action and as the message reappeared, froze the frame. He stared at the words, his excitement growing. Then he ran the commercial forward, counting twenty more frames with the identical message before the spot ended.

He hurriedly viewed five more DVDs, finding the same twenty-one subliminal frames on two. If the ratio held true, forty percent of the commercials carried a message aimed at altering the outcome of the election.

With Bacalla and Roland in hiding, there had to be at least one other person involved. But how many were there? Carter remembered his father's addendum to Murphy's Law: "There's always one more son-of-a-bitch than you counted on."

Carefully, Carter repacked the discs. As he sealed the last, he heard the door to the Media Center open. He threw the envelope into the cart and switched off the equipment.

At the far corner of the room was a closet. He focused on the position and killed the lights. Placing a hand on the cart to avoid it, he took huge, quiet strides across the darkness and felt for the door handle. Mercifully, the door wasn't locked. He stepped inside and pulled it shut.

His back pressed against the metal shelves behind him, Carter heard the studio door open and footsteps on the carpet. He heard the click of the switch and saw a shaft of light appear beneath the closet door.

Someone moved about the studio. Carter heard the rustle of cardboard envelopes as the intruder shuffled the contents of the cart. He hoped the envelopes he'd opened would go unnoticed.

Footsteps approached the door. Carter pressed himself against the shelves and raised his hands chest high. If the door swung open, he wanted as much room as possible to fight . . . or run.

Instead of opening, the door remained closed and Carter heard the lock click.

He was trapped.

73

11:36 a.m.

Rosie D and I were at her kitchen table when the telephone intruded on our conversation.

Rosie walked to the white phone on her kitchen wall.

"You've reached Rosie D," she said. Her phone greeting was one of the colorful mannerisms I had noticed. No one could accuse Rosie of lacking personality.

She listened for a moment, then handed me the phone. "Matt Carter. On his cell phone; he's locked up somewhere."

"Matt, what's going on?"

Carter explained what had happened, right up to finding Rosie Dombroski's number through information. "Darcy," he said, "you've got to get me out of here."

"Hang on. I'll call Garry."

***

Twenty minutes later the security guard, Garry Kaminski behind him, opened the closet door to a blinking Matt Carter.

"Thanks." Carter stood rubbing his eyes. "Well, I guess I've got the proof you need."

But the cart full of DVDs had disappeared. Kaminski's face showed his skepticism.

"I swear, Kaminski, there were two hundred DVDs in a cart right there. I ran five on the equipment and two contained subliminal messages."

"Yeah? What kind?"

"Just two words: Vanbuhler and leadership. Twenty-one times in each commercial, seconds apart."

"If the DVDs aren't here, where did they go?"

"Whoever locked me in the closet took them."

Kaminski turned to the young security guard. "Who's been here this morning?"

"Just Carter. I haven't seen another soul."

"Could anyone get in without you seeing?"

"There's a back door. I suppose someone could have come in through the mailroom, down the hall and up the freight elevator."

"Who has keys to the back door?"

"Not many people. The security staff. Don Rotunda, he's head of the mailroom. Maybe a few executives. Everyone else has to come and go through the glass doors in the front of the building."

"Which executives?"

"The list's downstairs."

"Let's see it. And let's look around for that mail cart."

A search of the building proved futile. The list of executives with keys to the back door was longer than the guard had remembered: a dozen people had keys. The security guard was writing a note recommending the changing of the lock when Kaminski and Carter left the building shortly after three.

74

Sunday evening

Sean, Garry, Rosie D and I sat in Rosie's living room, devouring two large pepperoni pizzas and chewing over our predicament. Much of the room's illumination came through the window from the yellow lights of the tall buildings a few blocks away.

I had lost interest in the pizza and concentrated on convincing my ex-husband that, with a bit more time, we could find evidence proving our innocence.

"Garry, you can see how close we are. You've got to give us another twenty-four hours."

Garry played the hard-ass cop, sitting silent in one of the two large light blue easy chairs, an empty paper plate on his lap. His chin rested in his hands and he wore one of those stubborn looks I'd come to know all too well during our brief period of so-called wedded bliss.

"What do you think, Garry? That Matt Carter locked himself in that closet? That all of this is our imagination?"

"No, Darcy, I don't think you're imagining anything. I'm imagining my career is on the line. I could lose everything I've worked for. On the other hand, if I take you in, you'll have every chance to tell your story . . . to people who can do more than I can."

"One thing they can do more of, is throw us in jail."

"Darcy, I want to help, believe me. But I need assurance there's a chance of proving your story."

It was time to bring AVC's top-secret project out of the garage. The Ampere debut hadn't seemed important to our situation until now. But maybe, just maybe, it represented a chance to catch the people behind our nightmare. I began describing A & B's confidential plans, watching for Sean's reaction. To my relief, he jumped in with details of his own.

When we concluded with the Ampere introduction tomorrow night and the airing of the new commercial, Garry sat staring at us, chin still resting on his hands. Rosie D saved the day.

"Garry, how can you sit there with your head up your butt when this whole thing is so obvious?"

Garry's head shot up, his chin coming off his hands.

"Why, everybody in the country's going to be watching that game tomorrow night. Isn't it perfectly clear they're going to run one of those . . . those sub-whatever commercials."

I could have kissed her. Whether because of Rosie's prompting, or some underlying desire to believe in me, Garry began to nod his head.

"Is there any way to get a look at the exact copy of the commercial they'll be airing?"

A call to Matt Carter indicated there was. Maybe. If it were scheduled for telecast from the Media Center at half time, the commercial would most likely be logged in tomorrow morning. Carter was confident he could sneak Garry in to view it during lunch hour break.

75

I still can't explain what happened later when Garry and Rosie D left Sean and me alone.

Maybe it was the frustration, the situation, the fact we had our backs to the wall. But, as we found ourselves alone in Rosie's apartment, the atmosphere suddenly became tense, awkward and extremely uncomfortable.

It was difficult to figure why. We had spent five days together up north. Outside of kissing, nothing sexual had gone on between us. Absolutely nothing.

Yet, the minute the door closed, I felt like a ninth grader on my first date. Tongue-tied, halting in my speech, tripping over myself. I would have felt more comfortable addressing AVC's Board of Directors naked than to find myself here, alone with the man I found so captivating.

At first, I told myself my attraction to Sean Higgins was simply a product of our situation: two people thrown together, shut away from the rest of the world. But now, I wasn't so sure. My feelings seemed more and more like the real thing.

And now, as we were finding our relationship had depth, it had no time. My ex-husband had given us twenty-four hours to come up with proof of our true but highly improbable story. If we failed, we would spend the next twenty years or more in prison.

This could very well be our last night together.

I confess. I suggested we adjourn to Rosie D's bedroom, where we experienced a slow, deliberate love making that each of us found immensely satisfying.

When we finished, we talked, wrapped comfortably in each other's arms. We spoke of our pasts. We shared experiences and talked of hopes for the future, when and if this experience ended. Each of us listened intently as the other spoke, hungry to know more.

During a pause, Sean leaned over and kissed me. As the kiss lingered, I began to explore his mouth again with my tongue.

"Does this mean the conversation is coming to a close?"

"Just postponed."

Our limbs intertwined one more time, and I felt Sean's body press tightly against mine. We were soon lost in an enjoyment of each other, better even than the first.

We both knew if tomorrow went wrong, this could well be the last time we made love.

76

Monday, Oct. 25—8:48 a.m.

The white-haired man nodded at the smiling flight attendant, stepped through the doorway of the plane, down the narrow tunnel, and into the bustling McNamara Terminal of Detroit's Metropolitan Airport.

Anyone who saw him leave Detroit little more than a week ago would have difficulty recognizing him. He had aged twenty years: his mustache gone, his straight black hair now snow white. His hairline had been shaved back three inches to the top of his head. Contact lenses turned his brown eyes brilliant blue, and he wore rimless spectacles. He stood two inches taller, thanks to lifts in his Italian loafers.

People passing the elderly, kind looking gentleman toting a small black bag would have guessed him a doctor. He attracted no more attention than he had leaving Washington's

Dulles Airport earlier that morning. There, he had passed easily through security even though the weapon he carried rivaled any pistol in its ability to inflict death. Inside the black bag rested a vial of the poison ricin, a KGB favorite. Fused with an oleomargarine base, it formed a combination so deadly that an untraceable amount would provoke a massive heart attack, while leaving no clue in the body of the victim. It was the poison that had killed Darren Cato.

Outside the terminal, the man shivered in the cold rainy October day. He cursed the United States and its weather. Pulling his coat tight around him, he waved down a courtesy van to take him to his waiting rental car.

77

11:34 a.m.

The blood red Dodge Intrepid stopped dead in the narrow cement driveway of a two-story brick home on Detroit's near east side. The white-haired man emerged from the car, the small black bag in one hand, a paper sack in the other.

Roland answered the knock, but not until the man spoke his name did he know who stood on his front porch.

"Damn, Bacalla, your own mother wouldn't recognize you."

The visitor maintained his deadpan expression as he walked past Roland into the sparsely furnished living room.

"I hope you came to get me the hell out of here," Roland said. "I'm tired of baby-sitting that damn Russian. I can barely understand a word he says."

The white-haired man ignored the comment. The Russian had served them well, but had also served his purpose. He would be taken care of, today. Andre Kursov, a world-renowned authority on the science of subliminal persuasion, had used the method to cure drug addicts, and his work had been reported in virtually every international medical journal. When funds for research ran low in his native country, it took little to persuade him to continue his work in the United States. Here major television networks were his laboratories, American voters his guinea pigs.

"Are the Ampere dubs taken care of?" the white-haired man asked.

"Yeah, yeah. I took Kursov to the agency, and your friend there did the rest. Got him into the Media Center to fix the duplicate DVDs. Had some trouble, though. That young producer stumbled over the finished product inside the control room. But that's taken care of. No one's going to find them where they're at now. And they go to the stations Tuesday morning."

"Very good. Here, I brought this." The man handed Roland the brown bag. He opened it and extracted a fifth of Johnny Walker Red. His hands began to shake.

"Thanks, thanks," he repeated, eyes glued to the bottle. "Scotch, not whiskey, but it'll do." Roland laughed to himself. "Yeah, it'll do just fine."

He headed for the kitchen, breaking the seal and screwing off the cap as he walked. He found an empty glass on the counter and poured it full. He took a drink, then others in rapid succession.

The white-haired man watched for a moment, then walked across the small living room and into the bedroom. He closed the door carefully and locked it. He set the black bag on the bed and went to the closet. Reaching up and as far back as he could, he withdrew a nine-millimeter pistol. He reached again and his hand felt the silencer. He attached it to the pistol barrel.

No hurry. He'd wait until tonight to make his move: to kill Manny Rodriguez in his hospital room. Then it would all be done. Niles VanBuhler would be elected President of the United States, and they could return to Mexico knowing the border would soon be open to the drugs that poured billions of dollars into the three major Mexican drug cartels. He laughed to himself. Mendoza and Lobo. The Monster and the Wolf. Soon they would be back home. They had done their job well.

78

When the American President declared war on narcotics, doubling the country's efforts to block drug trafficking along the U.S.-Mexican border, the Arellano Felix brothers who ran the Tijuana cartel declared war on President David Nordstrum. They sent for the man whose name was spoken in whispers.

Mendoza. *The Monster.*

The only son of an affluent Marxist lawyer, Ernesto Mendoza had been born in Colombia. His mother died when he was six. A rebellious youth, ignored by a father more dedicated to his causes than to his only son, he joined a gang at ten and killed a man by the time he reached the age of fourteen.

Mendoza's father sent him to the Jesuit school in Bogota where his IQ tested at 182. A brilliant student, but an incessant problem, he skipped school and harassed his teachers constantly. He was accused, but never convicted, of killing an instructor who failed him. He left the school shortly afterward.

He traveled to Europe, living for a while in London. Proficient in half a dozen languages by his twenty-third birthday, he found his way to the Patrice Lumumba University in Moscow, notorious training ground for Third World terrorists and future KGB agents. By the time he reached thirty, he found himself in demand as a paid assassin on three continents. Soon afterward, he settled in Colombia, becoming personal assistant, bodyguard and confidant to Pablo Escobar, head of the Medellin cartel. There, he met Lobo.

Lobo had been a child of the streets, born out of wedlock to a mother who died giving him birth. He, too, had learned to kill early, and was employed as a bodyguard to Pablo Escobar. At twenty-five, Mendoza became his mentor. Mendoza saw himself in the younger man, the way Lobo killed without remorse, and schooled him in the arts of terrorism.

In 1993, Pablo Escobar sent Mendoza to assassinate the head of the Cali drug family. The day Mendoza left Medellin, Escobar himself was gunned down by Colombia's anti-drug forces. His death caused a shift of power, with the Cali drug cartel now dominating the South American narcotics trade. Lobo found work with them, but when word of Mendoza's intent to assassinate the head of the Cali family leaked out, it forced the man they called "Monster" to flee to Europe.

During the early nineties, the Cali cartel depended on the Mexicans to smuggle cocaine across the U.S. border, then hand it over to their representatives in the United States. At first, they paid the Mexicans in cash, then in cash and cocaine. This opened an entirely new avenue to the Mexicans; they began to trade in cocaine independently.

By the late nineties, with most of the Cali leadership in prison, the balance of drug activity shifted to Mexico. Lobo followed, finding work with the notorious Arellano drug family. Their Tijuana organization ranked as the second largest drug cartel in the country, and the most vicious. Lobo soon became chief bodyguard for Ramon Arellano.

President Nordstrum's action in sealing off the border sent the Arellano family's revenues into freefall. Lobo suggested calling in Mendoza from Europe to assassinate Nordstrum. But Mendoza arrived in Mexico armed with a different plan.

"Assassinate the American president, and you will make him a martyr," he said. "Nordstrum's anti-drug policies will be cemented in place. You must make certain he is not re-elected."

"But how can we do that?" Arellano asked. "Supporting a candidate in an American election is very expensive. It cost us thirteen million dollars just to ensure the election of Niles VanBuhler, a congressman from a small district in California."

"I am not talking about simply supporting a candidate," Mendoza said. He told them of the work of Andre Kursov, the Russian expert in subliminal persuasion under whom he had studied at Patrice Lumumba University. The Russians had begun with the discoveries of the Americans' MKULTRA Project and built on them with experiments that made the CIA program seem like a tea party. Parents had been programmed to kill their children, and visa versa. But there had been positive results too: Mendoza described how Kursov cured patients with drug addictions by inserting messages into the videos they watched.

"Americans too have an addiction," Mendoza told Arellano. "They are addicted to television. But instead of curing that addiction, we will use it to our advantage."

79

Ramon Arellano called a meeting of the three major cartels, the families that ran the Mexican drug trade. Ramon and his brothers Carmen and Thomas of the Tijuana cartel attended, along with three members of the Fuentes family of the Juarez-based Chihuahua cartel, and Juan Garcia Abrego representing the Matamoros Gulf cartel.

The seven sat in the back room of one of Tijuana's finest restaurants, a room with white walls, white cabinetry and a snow white linen cloth covering the large oval table in the center. They wore expensive suits and handmade shoes, smoked hand-rolled Cuban cigars and eyed each other with suspicion.

In a drawing room just outside the door their bodyguards waited, watching each other with the same cold expressions.

In normal times, this meeting could never have taken place. These were men who coveted each other's territories, and would kill each other gladly to obtain them. But these were not normal times. The American President had to be dealt with and they had come to hear Ramon Arellano's plan.

Arellano rose to speak. David Nordstrum would be defeated in the next election, one year away. Further, their own candidate, California congressman Niles VanBuhler, would be elected.

Arellano called on Mendoza who spoke of the Russian Kursov and his work in subliminal persuasion. He described a plan to spread subliminal messages through the commercials of a large American advertising firm.

Mendoza's talk generated a predictable degree of skepticism and arguments from strong-willed men not accustomed to working together. But in the end, they embraced Mendoza's plan as the sole alternative to watching their money drain away.

The meeting broke up with the leaders of the two other cartels agreeing to take part in Arellano's scheme. They had heard the stories about Mendoza, and had confidence in his ability to execute the plan. But none of them, not even Arellano, knew that Mendoza had plans of his own. As the person responsible for VanBuhler's election, he would have a strong influence on the man. With President VanBuhler in his pocket, Mendoza - not Arellano or the others - would in time control the flow of all illegal drugs from Mexico into the United States.

Ordinarily, Mendoza insisted on working alone. But he recognized a plan this ambitious called for the help of others, men he could trust. He suggested Arellano lend him his bodyguard, his friend and former pupil, Lobo. Lobo had been an apt student who had mastered three languages in addition to Spanish, and had become nearly as adept as Mendoza at disguise.

Alone, each stood as a master of his craft. Together, they would be unstoppable.

80

I waited anxiously in Garry's apartment for news from the Media Center. Sean and Garry had joined Matt Carter to examine the master DVD of the Ampere commercial scheduled to debut this evening.

When Sean and Garry finally returned, I read the bad news on their faces.

"We played the Ampere commercial frame by frame," Sean said. "Nothing."

"Are you sure?"

"Sure? Of course I'm sure." He took a deep breath and collapsed on the couch. "I'm sorry, Darcy. It seemed so obvious VanBuhler's people would use tonight's game to telecast another message."

Garry cleared his throat. "More bad news. I got a call from Homicide on my way back.

"They found two bodies near your uncle's cabin. They also found the Avatar, painted white. They know you're driving a blue Chevrolet Lumina registered to your uncle, and they're looking for it here."

"Damn!" Sean echoed my feelings.

Garry looked at us with the expression of a man who had walked five miles with a stone in his shoe. "You're the major suspects in four murders now, and the net's getting tighter by the minute."

"Those DVDs scheduled for shipment to the stations are our only hope," I said. "We've got to find them."

"I said they're tightening the net, Darcy. The game's up."

"Damn it, Garry. If VanBuhler's elected it'll open a spigot of drugs pouring onto the streets. You were a narc. Think of the crime rate, not to mention the danger it'll mean to cops doing your old job. We've got to find those DVDs."

Garry looked like he might be weakening. I stared him down.

"Midnight. You've got until then. But you've got to promise to surrender voluntarily if we don't find anything."

I glared at him.

"I need your word."

"Alright, damn it. You have it." I flopped on the couch. "Now, let's figure out how we're going to get to the person who knows where those DVDs are."

Sean turned to Garry. "The keys: did building security give you a list of people with keys to both back door and Media Center?"

"Yeah, and I cross-checked both lists. Twenty people have keys to the back door, twelve have keys to the Media Center. Just eight have keys to both."

"Who are they?" Higgins asked.

Garry took out a small piece of paper from the breast pocket of his gray sport coat.

"Sid Goldman, Joe Adams, Michelle Ryder, C. J. Rathmore, Baron Nichols, Jonathon Goff, Sean Higgins, here, and Ken Cunningham."

"Michelle Ryder's been in Europe for the past month," Sean said.

Garry looked up. "That leaves seven suspects."

"C'mon," said Sean, "it leaves six. You don't think I . . ."

"Of course not," I said. "And you can't tell me Ken Cunningham or Sid Goldman are involved either. Or Joe Adams. Or . . ."

"You can't have it both ways," Garry said. "If your story is true, one of these people is guilty as hell. If you want to stay out of prison, you'd better find out who deserves to be there."

"What about the people who have keys to one or the other?" I asked.

"With five hundred employees, you've got five hundred potentials. Midnight's the deadline. These eight people are your best shot."

"Great," Sean Higgins chimed in at his sarcastic best. "Why don't we just find out who he is and get him to lead us to the DVDs?"

"I've got a better idea," I said. "Let's get him to lead us to the DVDs and then find out who he is."

81

The concept was as old as time: fight fire with fire.

The technology, as new as today: subliminal persuasion.

Management planned to telecast the Ampere commercial continuously on the lobby's closed circuit TV after it aired at halftime. We would plant a subliminal message warning that the DVDs scheduled for shipment had been discovered and "must be moved." That message would be meaningful to only one person: the SOB who knew the compromised Ampere DVDs existed.

Carter had recognized the technique used on the tainted Ampere discs and said our young computer wizard Jimmy Klein could plant the message "in his sleep." He'd sneak Jimmy into the Media Center during the crew's dinner break from five to six o'clock.

The trick: making sure we could follow the guilty party to the DVDs once he took the bait. With Michelle Ryder in Europe, six suspects remained, but just four of us to watch them. The plan I suggested had Sean and Garry watching the side door from the parking lot. As usual the front doors would be locked to discourage party crashers. That left the back door where Carter would be watching from his car for anyone trying to exit that way.

I would sneak into one of the offices looking down over the lobby. The lights off, I'd be invisible from below, but have a clear view of the proceedings. We'd keep in touch via cell phones. When the guilty person made a move, one of us would inform the others.

Or so the plan went. If it failed, Sean and I would have a lifetime to figure out why.

82

3:54 p.m.

The noise from the television on the bedroom dresser appeared as a whisper to the white-haired man seated on the bed. He concentrated on the events planned for the evening. The nine-millimeter Glock, silencer attached, lay beside him on the white bedspread.

When Mendoza and Lobo arrived in the United States earlier that year, they had brought two others, both Americans, former military men, who on occasion performed unauthorized wet work for the CIA. They had no allegiances and were for hire to the highest bidder. One, Frank Leath, had recently been sent to northern Michigan to take out the James woman and her boyfriend. The same agency-wide wiretaps that betrayed Caponi and Cato, had revealed the couple's hiding place. The other American, J. R. "Jack" Roland, decorated Gulf War soldier, bounced around Central and South America for a decade as a mercenary. Lately he had acquired an obsession for alcohol that turned him from a fighting demon to a man fighting demons within. Roland disguised his weakness, and by the time his addiction had been recognized, it was too late. Killing the policeman had been unnecessary and attracted unwanted attention.

A noise outside the door returned the white-haired man to the present. He opened the door to find Roland lurching about the small front room. Roland had gotten one arm in an overcoat and was attempting to pull it around his back.

"Leaving?"

"For another bottle. One you brought's gone."

The white-haired man put his hand on Roland's shoulder and guided him from the door. "You'll get your bottle," he said. "First, I want you to kill the Russian."

Roland's eyes lit up.

"Where is your gun?"

"Right here." Roland patted the front pocket of his trousers.

"I want you to go to the basement and shoot him twice in the head."

"You got it."

The white-haired man waited for the gunshots. When they came, he walked to the stairwell door and pulled it open. Roland stood at the bottom of the stairway.

"No problem," he said, starting up the stairs.

Roland got no farther than the fourth step. A quiet *poof* slid from the silencer as the man at the top of the stairs shot him once between the eyes.

"No. No problem at all."

83

5:14 p.m.

Kaminski wanted to be present when Jimmy Klein inserted our subliminal message and it didn't take a master detective to figure why my ex-husband insisted Sean go too.

He wanted to make it impossible for Sean and me to take off together.

The two left for the A & B Building just after four-thirty, so when the telephone rang a half hour later, it surprised me that the caller I.D. pinpointed the source as Homicide Headquarters, 1300 Beaubien. Had Garry changed his mind and turned Sean in?

I lifted the receiver. "Garry?"

"It's Joe Washington, his partner. This Rosie D?"

The last thing in the world we needed: Garry's partner finding out he hid a fugitive.

"Sure is." I did my best Rosie D impersonation. The recipe called for heaping tablespoons of enthusiasm.

"Kaminski's forever talkin' about you, Rosie. Hope we meet someday."

"Me, too. Garry's not home, Joe. Something I can do for you?"

"Just ask your fiancé if the invite to watch tonight's game there is still on. Have him call me at headquarters. I'll be here until eight."

"I'll let him know, Joe."

Two thoughts occurred to me. The first and most obvious: there was no way Garry's partner could come here. The second: with Bacalla on the loose and events coming to a head, Manny Rodriguez's life was very much in danger. He needed a bodyguard at the hospital more than ever. Joe Washington needed a place to watch tonight's game, and there were TVs in every hospital room I ever visited.

I waited five minutes before calling Washington back. Falling into my Rosie D impression, I told him I relayed his message to Garry and he had asked a favor.

"I owe him, Rosie. Name it."

I told him Garry wouldn't be home to watch the game because of a friend who had suddenly taken ill, and he worried about another friend who was in a coma. Would Washington stand guard at Henry Ford Hospital until Garry could take over?

"It would be a big favor, Joe," I said. "The man in the coma is a friend. His wife knocked him unconscious with a frying pan and Garry's afraid she might come back to do even more harm."

I sensed Washington's disappointment. "Oh, Rosie," he moaned. "Not tonight." It took some talking, but in the end

Washington agreed to watch Monday Night Football in Rodriguez's hospital room. But only until the game ended.

"I can't get there 'til seven fifteen or so," he said.

"Thanks, Joe, I'm sure that'll be fine."

I hung up and called Rosie D to ask if I could borrow her car.

"Certainly. But, it's not a car, it's a truck. Do you mind?"

Not if it has wheels.

Rosie expressed curiosity about her pickup's destination, so I told her. Concerned that I was putting myself in danger, she volunteered to go along. I used logic to talk her out of it. The "no visitors" sign was still up for Manny's room, and one person had a better chance of getting past the nursing staff than two. In the end, Rosie agreed, but when I came by to pick up the keys, she made me promise to take along a pistol Garry had given her for protection. I'm not crazy about guns, but since it would make Rosie feel better, I agreed. The small, nine-millimeter Beretta fit comfortably in the palm of my hand.

"I wouldn't be giving you this if I didn't have confidence in you," Rosie D said. She'd heard I had shot a man at Lake Manuka.

She had a hell of a lot more confidence in my ability to use the gun than I did.

84

I found Rosie D's blue Ford pickup fifty feet from the front door. Twelve minutes later, I pulled off Poe Street into emergency parking at Henry Ford Hospital.

Clouds had hung overhead like a dark, wet blanket all day. Rain fell now, and a dense fog cloaked the parking lot. Lights from the windows of the Clara Ford Pavilion on my left pierced the mist with an eerie yellow glow. Halloween loomed just around the corner and tonight seemed tailor-made for ghosts and goblins.

The fog hugged me on all sides, making it seem like walking through a narrow tunnel. Fine cold drops of mist settled against my face and my footsteps beat against wet pavement. Shivering, I pulled my dark green knee-length coat around me, tightened the belt and plunged both hands into the pockets. A scarf protected my head and ears from the chill.

The thought of Bacalla on the loose prompted another shiver that had nothing to do with the damp, cold air. The bastard enjoyed killing for the thrill and seemed to have an uncanny premonition of the future.

How had he known Vince Caponi, Darren Cato and Manny Rodriguez knew the secret of the Avion DVD? Did he suspect Sean and I also knew? Did he know the man sent to kill us at the Gaylord cottage had failed? If he did, how long before he came after us again?

I told myself to relax, but began to finger the pistol in my pocket, wondering if I had the nerve to use it.

* * *

Manny's room was four-eighteen, and as I neared it, a new worry struck home. What if Manny had visitors? The sign on his door clearly warned against it, but what if someone from the agency had come anyway?

Luckily, my concerns proved unfounded. The room was dark, the only light coming from the hallway behind me. I could just make out a shape in the bed. Not until I stood immediately beside it did I know for certain it was Manny Rodriguez. He seemed to be sleeping, a pained expression masking his face. He was a long way from the jovial Manny I remembered.

The apparatus Sean described had been removed, but as my eyes adjusted to the darkness, I noticed a tube in his right arm.

"Manny?" I reached down and touched his arm through the covers.

His eyes opened, at first staring blankly at the ceiling, then locking on my face. I thought I detected a smile.

"Manny? Do you hear me?"

He nodded. "Yes . . . weak."

"We know about the DVD . . . why you were beaten." Another nod.

"Can you move?"

Looking down, I could see his left arm move beneath the cover.

I removed my scarf and coat and set them on the chair between the bed and window. "It's lucky you're alive. There's going to be a policeman guarding you tonight."

"Policeman?"

"The people who did this to you, we want to make sure they can't hurt you again.

"I brought this." I reached over and took the pistol out of my coat pocket. I held it out. Manny smiled as he recognized the weapon.

The room suddenly grew darker and I looked up to see the silhouette of a large person standing at the door. A nurse making the rounds. I brought the pistol down quickly and, lifting Manny's head, shoved it under the pillow. I hoped she hadn't seen the gun.

She hadn't. The nurse walked to the foot of Manny's bed and reached for the chart.

That's when she noticed me. "I'm sorry, you'll have to leave. The patient's condition is still critical."

"But I'm an old friend." I stayed in the shadows.

"Doctor's orders." She turned toward the light switch. "I'll see you out."

I couldn't chance letting the nurse see my face. I grabbed my coat and scarf and, head down, started for the door.

"Don't trouble yourself." I brushed past the woman. In the hallway, I walked quickly to the elevator.

Not until the doors closed and the elevator headed for the main floor did I remember the pistol, still buried beneath Manny's pillow.

85

8:01 p.m.

Staring down from the darkened third floor office, the bright Adams & Benson lobby reminded me of a bustling beehive.

With the season's biggest football game an hour away, two teams were buzzing around, making last minute preparations. The ESPN-TV crew frantically checked cables, lighting and microphones for the remote telecast at halftime. The other team, A & B hourly employees on overtime, flew around hanging brightly colored team pennants all over the lobby, checking on refreshments and fine-tuning sound equipment that would broadcast the game to every corner of the lobby. The workers had to maneuver around a few early celebrants who had crashed the party prior to the official eight-thirty opening and stood chatting and drinking.

With everyone focused on the evening's preparations, sneaking up to the third floor had been the proverbial piece of cake. I had been caught on video of course; there were security cameras all over. But unless a reason popped up to replay the discs, say a burglary somewhere in the building, their contents would never be reviewed.

Bleachers had been erected to face giant forty-foot screens installed at either end of the lobby. To my right, the north end was covered in green and white New York Jets pennants and banners; the south end decked out in the familiar red and gold of the San Francisco Forty-Niners.

The receptionist's desk had been removed from the center of the lobby and replaced with a round platform about three feet high. Atop that sat a canvas-covered shape the length, width and height of a small vehicle. Lines ran from the canvas shroud to the ceiling. At the right moment during halftime, the canvas would be lifted, introducing the new Ampere to the people here, and to a national television audience at home. Two beefy security men stood on either side of the platform, making sure party guests didn't help themselves to a preview.

Besides the giant screens at each end, at least twenty smaller monitors had been positioned about the lobby. There were a half dozen portable bars, and a number of stands with colorful signs boasting they served pizza, hot dogs and Italian sausage sandwiches.

Tonight, tonight . . . won't be just any night . . .

Steven Sondheim's lyrics blending with Leonard Bernstein's melody poured through my mind like water from a faucet I couldn't shut off. I'd spent untold afternoons at the piano absorbed in the score of *West Side Story*, despite the fact it had been popular two decades before I was born.

Tonight would *not* be just any night. It couldn't be. Tonight had to be the night the madness stopped.

A knot of nervousness tied itself in the pit of my stomach, accompanied by a pounding in my temples. *Not a headache. Not now.* I rubbed the sides of my head.

My watch read eight-o-seven. I pictured Joe Washington on his way to Henry Ford Hospital. He'd split immediately after the game, but it was better than nothing. By then this nightmare would be over . . . one way or another.

Tonight, tonight . . .

86

10:16 p.m.

"How long you figure this thing'll take to work?" Kaminski took a sip from his coffee mug.

He and Higgins sat in an unmarked Taurus in the Adams & Benson lot. The game played on the radio; the Jets up fourteen to seven with minutes to go in the half.

"Damned if I know," Higgins shrugged. "This subliminal crap is new to me, too."

They had found a parking spot fifty feet from the side entrance. With all other doors locked, they had a clear view of everyone coming and going.

"It better be one of those six," Kaminski said. "With two hundred people inside, we sure as hell can't follow everyone."

That, Higgins thought, is the biggest hole in the whole damn plan. Instead of saying so, he stared out the car window at a brightly lit ore freighter sliding past the city on its way south.

10:43—p.m.

I had forgotten about the football game until a roar from the lobby caused me to look at the giant screen on my left in time to see a Jets player doing his version of the hula in the end zone. The numbers on the screen told the score: twenty-one to seven, New York.

Big deal. Since the opening kickoff my attention had been focused on the crowd. Thankfully, every one of our six suspects was there. Joe Adams arrived first, followed shortly by Ken Cunningham. Forgive me, but I still couldn't imagine Ken Cunningham or Sid Goldman as suspects.

The others arrived soon after Cunningham. Sid appeared with his wife Mavis, followed by C. J. Rathmore, and Jonathon Goff, A & B's vice president of media. Baron Nichols came last, fashionably late at the end of the first quarter.

Looking down from the darkened office, I spotted Will Parkins and two guys from research in the Jets bleachers, still high-fiving after the New York touchdown.

I found Sid and Mavis Goldman in the Forty-Niners bleachers, Sid dressed in a well-worn Forty-Niners jacket. I remembered he had spent time at BBDO in San Francisco.

To one side of the bleachers, Paul Chapman stood by himself, taking in the scene. Ginny Stankowski, Glo-Jo Johnson, M. J. Curtis and a woman I didn't recognize stood beside one of the refreshment stands.

It seemed like a hundred years since we had all been together and I couldn't believe how much I missed the whole group.

In the center of the lobby, a few men wearing black jackets with the ESPN logo on the back began moving around a group of agency and AVC brass, testing lights and camera positions. In minutes the world would have its first look at the Ampere.

Next to the shroud-covered platform, I saw Ken Cunningham, Joe Adams and C. J. Rathmore with two American Vehicle VIPs: William Kesler and Malcolm Sears, AVC's Board Chairman and President. Carter told me Ken Cunningham would present a brief history of the development of the Ampere, then toss the ball to AVC Board Chairman Kesler for the actual introduction. On Kesler's cue, the canvas would lift, and the Ampere unveiled to the world.

The Ampere commercial with its subliminal and hopefully not-so-subliminal messages would follow.

87

11:01 p.m.

Toting the small black bag, the white-haired man had no trouble entering Henry Ford Hospital long after visiting hours. Most of the staff members he passed took him for a doctor on the way to his rounds.

Once on the fourth floor he encountered a predicament: a tall black man, no doubt a policeman, sitting just inside Rodriguez's room. Bacalla had noticed him in time to walk past and enter an empty room two doors away. He would wait to see how dedicated a sentry the policeman turned out to be. If he left to have a cigarette or visit the cafeteria on the first floor, Bacalla would strike. On the other hand, should the waiting become too tiresome, he would walk into the room posing as Rodriguez's physician and deliver the fatal injection while the policeman watched.

Either way the man in bed would die.

* * *

The Ampere introduction went smoothly.

I had a perfect view from the darkened office. As scripted, Cunningham spoke first and turned the microphone over to Bill Kesler.

Kesler hadn't uttered two sentences when it became painfully clear why Ken had been chosen to deliver the major portion of the program. Kesler was dull as dust. Mercifully, his verbal meandering lasted only moments. Then the canvas lifted toward the four-story ceiling, and the Ampere made its debut before an applauding Adams & Benson audience and millions watching at home.

The Ampere commercial followed and received a predictably enthusiastic reception in the lobby, since this marked the first time most A & B staffers had seen it. The spot then began running continuously on three monitors designated for that purpose.

I watched as people crowded around the monitors for a second and third viewing. To my delight, every person on our list drifted over for another look at one time or another.

If the plan took a dive, it wouldn't be because no one had been exposed to the subliminal message.

88

11:37 p.m.

The Jets broke the game open with three quick touchdowns in the third quarter, and the majority of people below me turned their attention to talking, eating and drinking.

Most of the American Vehicle Corporation brass left as the third quarter ended but Adams and Cunningham remained, mingling with employees.

I kept my eye on Joe Adams. There had been something unusual all evening: he hadn't consumed a drop of liquor. I watched intently each time he approached one of the bars. The bartender poured from a bottle of Vernor's Ginger Ale, never once reaching for whiskey. Even after the clients left, Adams nursed ginger ale straight up. By this time on most occasions he would have been poured into his car and driven home.

I decided to relay my observation to Sean and Garry, and punched the numbers to Sean's cell phone.

He answered on the first ring. "Yeah?"

"I've noticed something strange about Joe Adams. Is Garry there?"

"No." I could detect a smile in his voice. "He's down at the river taking a leak. He's been drinking coffee all night and it's his third trip. What's up?"

I explained my suspicions.

"I'll tell Kaminski. Keep your eye on Adams."

I did, and with the fourth quarter half over, Adams made a move. He began shaking hands, working his way toward the door. I phoned Sean again.

"Yeah?"

"Joe Adams is leaving. He'll be out the door in minutes."

"Got it. We're on him."

89

12:24 a.m.

It seemed an eternity since Joe Adams left and I hadn't heard from Sean or Garry.

With the outcome of the game decided long ago, the party below had begun breaking up. But five of the suspects still lingered in the lobby.

Tall, curly-haired Jonathon Goff stood in the center of a group of his media buyers enthralled with his every word. Agency parties made great opportunities for brownnosing the boss.

Ken Cunningham chatted with Tom Kuhn, A & B's Vice President of Research in front of one of the monitors displaying the Ampere commercial. I longed to go down and talk with Ken. He had been like an uncle while I was growing up, and he would know how to help.

The sound of the phone pierced my thoughts. I grabbed the receiver.

"Sean?"

"Darcy, listen to me. I'm in the back seat of Kaminski's car, under arrest. Cops are all around and I don't know how long I can talk."

"Did you find Adams?"

"We found him. He drove directly to his secretary's house in Grosse Pointe. She met him at the door dressed in a flimsy negligee. They're having an affair."

"What did Kaminski do?"

"What the hell do you think? He put me in the back seat of his car and called his office. He's standing outside right now."

"But Sean . . ."

"Kaminski just noticed me talking on the phone. He's coming for me. Run for it, Darcy or they'll get you . . ."

Kaminski's voice came on. "Darcy? Stay where you are, I'll be right there."

I slammed down the phone. My first thought: don't panic.

Down in the lobby, I saw Ken Cunningham and Tom Kuhn shake hands. As Kuhn went out the glass doors, Cunningham headed for a metal door fifty feet away that led to the basement of the building.

I had to talk with Ken, to explain what was happening. He'd know what to do.

I ran out into the hall to the elevator. Once on the ground floor, I kept to the outside wall of the lobby, walking quickly, trying to avoid the few stragglers left. I shielded the side of my face with one hand, probably unnecessarily. By this time most guests were too busy saying goodbyes and too far into their cups to notice me.

I reached the metal door without attracting attention. Flinging it open, I found a flight of metal steps running down into darkness.

At the bottom of the stairs I paused to let my eyes adjust to the dim light. I stood at the end of a long tunnel-like corridor. A string of dim yellow emergency lights positioned about twenty feet apart stretched along the ceiling as far as I could see.

I thought I heard footsteps straight ahead.

"Ken?" My voice echoed against cement walls.

"Ken?"

I began walking forward.

90

12:54 a.m.

Where the hell is Kaminski?

Joe Washington checked his watch for the fourth time in seven minutes, exactly the span since the game had ended.

It had been bad enough sitting through that runaway. Super Bowl replay? Bull. Wasn't even a contest past the second half kick off. But with the game on, at least he had *something*.

He glanced at the figure in the bed. Rodriguez had opened his eyes a few times during the game, mostly when the crowd noise grew loud. Washington almost expected him to talk.

Where the hell is Kaminski?

He got up and walked to the door, looking out. The hall deserted, he checked his watch again.

Twelve-fifty-five.

There hadn't been a sniff of trouble all night. Washington decided to give Kaminski until one o'clock.

Then he'd be the hell out of here.

91

12:56 a.m.

How long I had been picking my way through this cold, dark and seemingly endless maze of corridors, I didn't know. I lost track of time. I made a wrong turn somewhere and came to a dead end. Retracing my steps to the main hallway, I continued to follow the dim yellow emergency lights.

A cement wall loomed just ahead. *Lord, please, not another dead end.* As I neared the wall, I saw the corridor take a jog to the left. I followed and found myself standing outside a cavernous room. A freight elevator on the far side had several white canvas mail carts directly in front; carts used to hold outgoing mail; carts that might hold discs ready for shipment. I guessed the position of this room directly below the first floor mailroom.

A tall white-haired man stood next to one of the carts, his back to me.

"Ken?" The sound of my voice bounced around the room like a racquetball.

Startled, the man turned quickly. *Oh, Lord, no, not Ken. He couldn't be involved in this.* I walked toward him.

"Darcy? What the hell are you doing down here?"

"I was following you. Why are you here?"

"I . . . I came to check on packages that have to go out tomorrow."

I stood five feet from Ken, close enough to see drops of perspiration on his brow. In the faint light I saw the cart next to him full of discs in cardboard envelopes; there were at least two hundred.

It had to be the cart Riggs found in the Media Center yesterday.

"They're copies of the new Ampere spot," Cunningham said. "I . . . I thought they might . . . well, I just thought I ought to check on them."

"Why?" I knew the answer, but hoped the man I'd known since childhood would come up with something I hadn't considered: a simple, innocent reason for being here.

Cunningham wrinkled his brow, eyes darting about the room. He seemed to search for an answer. "I don't know exactly. I had this strange urge . . ."

"Maybe it was the same kind of urge people are getting to vote for Niles VanBuhler."

"What are you talking about?"

"Subliminal messages. In those commercials there, and in the Ampere commercial you saw tonight."

"Subliminal messages? That's crazy."

"We planted a message in the Ampere commercial that ran tonight, Ken. A message that would be meaningless . . . except to someone involved in the plot to influence next week's election.

"And damn it, Ken." My voice cracked, "That message led you here."

"Election? Message? Darcy, you'd better explain yourself."

I told him, starting with Caponi's murder and Cato's fake suicide, the beating of Manny Rodriguez, and Sean Higgins' discovery of the subliminal messages in Traverse City. When I finished, Cunningham appeared dumbfounded.

"Conspiracy? Here at Adams & Benson? I don't believe it."

"Believe it."

The third voice startled us both. I whirled to see the outline of a man in the doorway. Even in the dim light, there was no mistaking C. J. Rathmore.

And he held a pistol.

92

Tuesday, October 26—1:03 a.m.

Killing the policeman in Rodriguez's room would have been easy, perhaps even enjoyable, but the white-haired man waited him out.

Seated in an empty room two doors from Rodriguez, he heard the policeman leave. He waited two minutes then walked silently to the hall and peered out. To his right, at the far end of the corridor, he saw three nurses starting their rounds.

He ducked back into the room. He wanted no confrontation this night. No trouble. He looked forward to a quick kill, a few hours rest, and a plane home to Tijuana. He would wait those nurses out, too. The man two doors away wasn't going anywhere.

* * *

The nurse had come and gone. Manny Rodriguez lay gazing at the ceiling, wondering whether the vision of Darcy had been real.

He had regained consciousness days ago. But constantly drifting in and out of sleep, he found it difficult to separate dream from reality. At first he had no recollection of where he lay or how he had gotten there. He guessed a traffic accident, then a fall. Breathing hurt; probably broken ribs.

His legs remained numb, but his arms had movement. Each day since regaining consciousness he struggled to move them a bit more.

He overheard the nurses talking about a beating, but it took time to realize they referred to him. He had no memory of a beating or inkling of why anyone would want to hurt him.

He spent much time sleeping, as he had tonight. He knew the man who'd been there earlier had gone, but suddenly felt the presence of someone else. He tilted his head forward slightly, making out the outline of a man carrying some sort of bag. As the man came closer, he saw the hair on his head appeared white as snow.

He sensed something familiar about the man, perhaps someone he should know, someone from long ago. Then he felt another presence.

"May I ask what you're doing here?" Rodriguez recognized the voice of one of the nurses.

"I'm Doctor Orlich. I'm here to see this patient."

"I don't recall your name on our staff bulletins."

"I'm filling in. Short notice."

Rodriguez felt the weight of the bag near his feet as the man set it down. He heard the rasp of a zipper.

"What are you doing?" the nurse asked.

"The patient requires an injection." The white-haired man took something from the bag, a vial of liquid. He reached again and withdrew a syringe.

The nurse picked up the chart at the foot of his bed and began reading it. "I don't see where Doctor Logan prescribed an injection."

"I spoke with Dr. Logan half an hour ago. He said the patient has been restless."

"There is no Dr. Logan," the nurse said. "I made up the name. The patient's physician is Dr. Reiner."

"And you have outsmarted yourself." The man dropped the syringe onto the bed and grabbed the nurse with both hands. She tried to call out, but managed only muffled sounds. The man had his left hand on her mouth, holding her tight. With his right hand he reached for the syringe and plunged it into her neck.

The nurse went limp and he laid her on the floor. Rodriguez couldn't see the woman, but could hear her thrashing as if suffering a seizure or heart attack.

He felt helpless. He couldn't sit up, could barely move. Then he remembered the pistol. Darcy had pushed it under the left side of the pillow. His left hand lay at his waist. Struggling mightily, he moved it upwards three inches.

The nurse stopped thrashing and the stillness of death permeated the room. The man reached into his black medical bag and withdrew a second syringe. He lifted the vial.

Six more inches. Rodriguez struggled for inches, each movement of his hand a gargantuan accomplishment.

The white-haired man held the vial and syringe toward the ceiling. He drew the plunger back and filled the hypodermic with the liquid that sent the nurse into convulsions.

Three inches more.

Rodriguez worried whether he could lift the pistol once he reached it. It was light, a Beretta. He had fired thousands of rounds with this particular type of weapon. He knew the weight, the feel, the location of the safety, the exact amount of force to use on the trigger.

The white-haired man held the syringe toward the door and checked its contents. He turned and approached the bed, the syringe in front of him.

Rodriguez thrust his hand up, and under the pillow.

There it was.

If the white-haired man had noticed Rodriguez's movement in the darkness, he gave no indication. He reached with one hand and pulled off the covers, exposing Rodriguez's body. He bent down, and pulled up Rodriguez's hospital gown.

Summoning every bit of strength, Rodriguez pulled the Beretta from beneath the pillow and thrust it forward. The white-haired man looked up, his face going blank as he saw the gun. His eyes widened as the Beretta fired.

"You bastard," the man stammered. He staggered backward, hand to his right shoulder. He regained his balance and moved forward, the deadly hypodermic now in his left hand. The wound had slowed him, but he came closer just the same. Rodriguez recognized there was nothing more he could do, no way he could lift the gun again. Three feet from the bed, the man stumbled and fell forward, sprawling face down, the top of his head hitting Rodriguez's leg.

Dead? No.

The man fought his way back up, lifting himself on his elbows, then fell again.

It wasn't until he tried a second time: face straining, holding himself high, then collapsing on the bed, that Rodriguez knew the man with the snow white hair wasn't going to get up.

Not now or ever.

The syringe had lodged in his throat.

* * *

When the bullet first hit the white-haired man, he knew instinctively the wound in his shoulder was not fatal. A lifetime on the streets, killing, wounding and being wounded taught him enough to know he would recover.

But he hadn't counted on tripping over the dead nurse's leg and falling against the bed. As he struggled to raise himself and felt the sudden sensation of pain rush through his chest, he realized immediately what had happened. He knew that, for him, the fight had ended.

Mendoza and Lobo. Lobo and Mendoza. The team dissolved in a single awkward move.

Lobo lay dying; now it was up to Mendoza.

He knew the Monster would not fail.

93

1:07 a.m.

"Miss James, what a surprise. To paraphrase one of your American authors, the reports of your death have been greatly exaggerated."

"C. J., what the hell?" Ken's words trailed off. He began walking toward Rathmore.

"Stay there."

Cunningham stopped in his tracks. "C. J., what about these DVDs?"

"Miss James is correct." The yellow glare from the emergency lights reflected off the round lenses of Rathmore's glasses making it impossible to see his eyes and creating an appearance more sinister than the gun he pointed.

Ken turned to me. "I swear, Darcy, I had nothing to do with these DVDs. With you and Higgins gone, I've had to run the account. Rathmore asked me to store the discs where they wouldn't be found. But I had no idea . . ."

"No," Rathmore said. "You were the perfect dupe."

I asked, "Who are you? Who do you work for? Mendoza?"

A hollow laugh. "I am Mendoza."

A chill ran through me. "But the photograph of Mendoza the police uncovered resembles Robert Bacalla."

"Ah, the unfortunate photograph. The only one ever taken of either of us. The face is indeed the man you refer to as Robert Bacalla. In my country he is known as Lobo."

"But the authorities say Mendoza assassinated that government official."

"Yes. Lobo was there to cover my exit. In the picture I stood out of sight, directly behind him.

"Now I will ask the questions." Mendoza motioned to the pistol. "It is imperative you provide the correct answers."

Ken raised a clenched fist. "I'll be damned if I do another thing for you, Rathmore . . . Mendoza, or whatever the hell your name is."

The pistol in Mendoza's hand barked, and Ken fell to the floor. He rolled over screaming, holding his left knee with both hands.

"You son-of-a-bitch."

"I repeat: I will ask the questions . . . and shoot again and again if the answers are not correct."

I'd had enough of the bastard. "You're going to kill us anyway."

"Perhaps. But there are ways to die. Death can be quick, or you can beg me to end your pain.

"Now, who besides yourselves is aware of the message on the discs? And please think carefully before you answer; I will make it very unpleasant if you lie."

My head reeled. I couldn't block out the sounds Ken made, moaning with pain as he rolled on the cement floor. No one knew we were here, and I was the only one with the information Mendoza wanted.

If I gave him the names, the others—Higgins, Carter, Kaminski and Rodriguez would die along with Ken and me. The conspiracy would go undetected, and Mendoza and his people would control the government of the United States. Major cities plagued by drugs and drug-related crime just a few years ago would slip back into the morass. Somehow I had to deal with the pain. I couldn't let that happen.

"The names, please." Mendoza motioned with the pistol.

Cunningham glared, his face a mask of pain, fear and anger. "I don't know what you're talking about."

The gun barked again and Cunningham let out another yelp, this time clutching his right knee.

"Ken!" I cried. I couldn't help it, I couldn't bear seeing my friend suffer. "Ken, I'm so sorry." Immediately, I regretted letting Rathmore see my weakness.

"Mr. Cunningham apparently doesn't have the answers. But, Miss James, I know you do." Mendoza moved to Ken's writhing form on the floor. "I'll give you five seconds to tell me what I want to know, or the next bullet ends his life."

"Don't tell him, Darcy. Don't . . ." Ken fell over, passed out from pain and shock.

Baaammm!

I jumped as the explosion of a gunshot echoed through the empty room. It took a second to recognize it hadn't come from Mendoza's weapon.

Mendoza reacted with the spring of a jungle animal. Suddenly behind me, his arm reached around my throat, using me as a shield between him and the doorway fifty feet away.

"Whoever you are, give up your weapon and show yourself, or the woman dies."

Seconds passed. A gun came sliding across the cement floor. A moment later Garry Kaminski materialized from the darkness, hands over his head.

Why the hell did he surrender? Our last chance lay in his coming back with more cops. "Get out of here!" I screamed.

"Come here," Mendoza countered. "The woman dies in five seconds. One . . . two . . ."

Garry walked slowly toward us, stopping a few feet away. Mendoza recognized him immediately. My ex-husband had questioned him after Vince Caponi's death.

"Turn to the wall, Sergeant Kaminski. Spread your arms and legs." Mendoza pushed me away and faced Garry, now spread-eagled against the cement wall.

"I have heard police often carry a second weapon." Keeping a discreet distance behind my ex-husband Mendoza leaned in, running his hand up and down Garry's sleeves, and around his middle. He found nothing.

Mendoza kneeled and ran his hand down one leg, then the other. He smiled as he felt Garry's right ankle. Lifting the pant leg, he pulled a small pistol from the ankle holster.

"You policeman aren't so smart." He looked at me: "What is your connection to Sergeant Kaminski? You referred to him by his first name."

"I don't have to answer that, you bastard." If this man was going to kill us all, he sure as hell wasn't going to get the satisfaction of seeing me squirm.

"That woman is my former wife," Garry said suddenly. "Don't kill her. And please . . . please . . . don't kill me."

Garry? Whining? This from the tough cop I had been married to?

"So this is the kind of policeman you have in Detroit." Mendoza sneered. "Cowards."

"Don't shoot. Please don't shoot."

"Look, he's pissing his pants." Mendoza laughed and I saw a dark spot forming at the crotch of Garry's light chino trousers.

In the past, I sometimes wondered what went through the minds of people in the moment they realized they were about to die. Now I knew. A feeling of sheer terror. No pictures of my life flashing before my eyes. Instead, my heart pounded wildly in my chest, my throat felt dry and tight, like someone choking me.

"My pants. I'm peeing my pants." I felt sorry for my ex-husband. I once looked to the man as a hero, and now his reaction was making things worse. I felt terrified for myself, and embarrassed for him. The cops he worked with always talked about his nerve under fire.

As Garry unbuckled his belt, Mendoza reveled in the display.

"I can't stand the wet." Garry now unbuttoned his trousers.

"He's performing a strip for us," Mendoza said.

Garry's pants hung around his knees, and he reached into his under shorts. I had the horrible thought he would pull them off as well.

"He's going to take out his . . . his business."

"Here's my business." Garry's voice no longer a whine, but a growl. He yanked a pistol from his under shorts and fired it directly into Mendoza's face.

The bullet slammed through Mendoza's right cheek. As he fell, he managed to lift his gun and shoot.

To my horror I saw the last bullet Mendoza would ever fire had struck home. Garry fell backward, a spot of blood expanding rapidly across his white shirt.

"Garry! Garry!" I cried, running to him as he crumpled onto the cement floor.

Too late. He couldn't hear me.

EPILOGUE

A cool January breeze meandered across warm white sand, carrying welcome relief to tourists baking on the ocean side of the Xanadu Hotel.

The breeze found Darcy lying on a towel, face to the sun and eyes closed, wondering why everyone didn't spend January in the Bahamas. Here winter refused to intrude on crystal clear waters, sandy white beaches and warm moonlit evenings. Here waves could be heard stroking the shore every evening from a tenth story bedroom window. And words like *cold* and *snow* were as distant as the events of October.

The wedding had come off smashingly, and it would be another week before they were expected back at Adams & Benson.

The agency had taken over all American Vehicle Corporation business as of January first, and with Ken Cunningham still recuperating, the transition hadn't gone particularly smoothly. But Baron Nichols could handle it.

Getting the business had meant good and bad news for Nichols. The good news: he finally got his wish to head up an AVC creative team. He'd been appointed creative supervisor on Advancer sport utility and AVC pickups. The bad news, at least for him: he reported to Darcy James. She had been promoted to vice president, creative director, over the entire AVC account.

More good news: with the drug cartels' plot exposed and the truth behind the murders known, she and Higgins were looked upon as heroes, a major turnaround from October.

It had taken time for the evidence to reach the proper authorities, and for those in power to act. In fact, it hadn't happened soon enough.

Niles VanBuhler's election to the nation's highest office shocked political pundits who had given him no chance six months earlier. But the surprise of his election was nothing next to the shock that came days afterward when VanBuhler's deception was disclosed and he went from being hailed to jailed, as a traitor. He and running mate Reed Conley were currently free on bond and managing to stay clear of the national spotlight. It would be months before a trial date was even set. Darcy felt sorry for Conley, a former Congressman from North Carolina, who may have been innocent of any wrongdoing.

A week of political intrigue followed the election as the nation found itself without a President-elect. The Supreme Court resolved the issue with one of the most controversial decisions in its history. The Court voted five to four against a new election, awarding victory to David Nordstrum. Nordstrum had come within an eyelash of winning and few doubted he would have gained reelection had it not been for the cartel plot.

David Nordstrum's inauguration would take place just days from now. He called the cartels' action an "act of terrorism" and intended to announce, with the cooperation of the other countries involved, the expansion of America's war on drugs to include raids on cartel properties in Mexico and Central and South America.

The plot to guarantee VanBuhler's election had been a combination of genius and blind luck. Mendoza had carefully scripted the planting of subliminal messages, right up to importing the Russian expert; but discovering their candidate had a former college friend who headed a major advertising agency was pure good fortune. Once they uncovered Joe Adams' love for alcohol and gambling, the rest came easy.

VanBuhler arranged a weekend trip to the Bahamas, a friendly reunion of two old college buddies. Adams, delighted that his friend had named A & B to handle his advertising, took to the bait like a ravenous rainbow ravaging a fly. There followed a weekend of booze, broads and big time losses at the crap tables, courtesy of the Mexican connection. Gambling debts became the nail in Joe Adams' financial coffin that forced him to sell the agency his father had founded. The highest bidder, the British holding company Solomon & Solomon, turned out to be a laundering operation for Mexican drug money. Once the agency became the property of Solomon & Solomon, Bacalla, a.k.a. Lobo, took over as head of the VanBuhler team. The fact they had monitored agency telephones early explained a number of things. Intercepting Caponi's call to Darren Cato was one; pinpointing Darcy and Higgins' whereabouts in northern Michigan had been another. And once Bacalla learned of Darcy's suspicions, he had her home telephone monitored as well, overhearing the call that led to Manny Rodriguez's savage beating.

Not everyone on the VanBuhler staff was privy to the plot. Mendoza hired advertising and political professionals to carry on the day-to-day business of electing a third-party candidate, providing an effective front for his henchmen's activities.

But it was Kaminski who saved the day, and saved Darcy's life. Darcy learned the story from the security guard who led Kaminski downstairs to where she and Cunningham were held by Mendoza. Kaminski had left Higgins and returned to Adams & Benson to arrest her. He found no one in the lobby except a clean-up crew and the night security guard. The guard told him no one remained upstairs.

Kaminski had a sudden inspiration; he asked the guard to play the last fifteen minutes of a disc from one of the lobby security cameras. When he played the action in fast-forward fashion there they were: Cunningham, then Darcy and finally C. J. Rathmore crossing the lobby and entering the basement stairwell.

The security guard led Kaminski into the basement and through the labyrinth of halls to the large room. They heard voices as they approached. Looking in, Kaminski saw Cunningham on the floor, blood bubbling from his leg, Mendoza pointing the gun at Darcy. Kaminski quickly dismissed the idea of taking a shot from where he stood, fifty feet away. He had seconds to piece a plan together.

The pressure of a full bladder made it difficult to concentrate. He had spent the earlier part of the evening drinking coffee in his car, and was paying the price. But the discomfort gave him an idea.

Knowing he might be searched for a second gun, he borrowed the security guard's weapon, placing it in his ankle holster. He shoved the tiny Beretta he carried in his ankle holster into the crotch of his underwear. It was a high-risk plan, but all he had. He prayed that Rathmore wouldn't go near his crotch when patting him down.

The plan worked, right up to the time Kaminski took a bullet in the chest.

"Hey, Darcy. You gonna lie there all day? It's almost noon...time for a Bahama Mama."

Darcy opened her eyes to see Rosie D standing over her. She sat up, one hand shading her eyes. "Where's Garry?"

"Over at the drink tent, where'd ya think? Sean's meeting the three of us there for lunch."

The original wedding date had been mid-December, but Kaminski hadn't recovered enough to go through with it. They rescheduled the ceremony for January, and asked Darcy and Higgins to serve as Maid of Honor and Best Man. It was Rosie's idea that the two join them on their honeymoon.

Higgins had joked about making it a double wedding, but that's all it was: a joke. For Darcy, it was far too soon to know how she felt toward Sean. Time would tell, and right now she couldn't think of a better place to spend time.

"Okay, let's go," Darcy said. She and Rosie strolled toward the tent set up for the convenience of hotel guests who didn't want to stray from the sand and surf for lunch or drinks.

"Hey, Darcy."

Higgins came running toward her from the hotel, a huge smile covering his face. Reaching her, he picked her up, swung her around, and set her back down in the sand. He leaned forward and kissed her.

Darcy felt euphoric. Maybe it was the warmth of a perfect day, or the warmth of a relationship that seemed to grow more perfect by the day. Or perhaps it was the lifting of the dark veil of horror that covered them for so many days.

Whatever the reason, she couldn't remember being happier than right now, right here, at this moment.

Freeze frame.

Freeze Frame

Don't miss the next B. David Warner novel:

Dead Lock

Read the first two chapters . . .

1

June, 1943

The problem, Lyle Banner figured, wasn't the gunman or the hostage. It was the rotten timing.

You're a Lieutenant on the Detroit Police Force, you've faced this kind of situation before: a gunman holding some poor schnook hostage. The fact that the hostage is a popular reporter for the *Detroit Times* and the gunman is a mob hit man makes it even better. Play it smart and there could even be a promotion in it.

But not now. Not ten days from retirement. Screw this up, and the reputation you've nursed for thirty years goes into the tank like a trick pony off a high board.

Banner looked around, sizing up the situation for the nth time tonight. Half a dozen police cars parked side by side on the street, headlights trained on the reporter's white two-story house. The house, with its postage stamp cement porch and tiny front lawn, sat close to the street. The porch, sidewalk and grass were still damp from the rain that fell for a few minutes just after dark. The street had been cordoned off at both ends, and houses on either side of the reporter's evacuated. The crowd had grown steadily since the police cars arrived just before dark, and stood behind ropes three houses away on either side. The small group of people milling around inside the roped area included police, emergency personnel and a few reporters.

"They say stall him, Lieutenant."

Banner squinted toward his sergeant, John Wolenski, seated in the squad car six feet away. The car's two-way radio connected them with the Chief of Police and his staff downtown.

"Stall him? Stall him? A mob killer's demanding a car and a thousand dollars cash, and that's the best they can do?"

Banner went on. "I can see them around that table in the Chief's office right now, figuring what they're gonna say when everything blows up in my face. Which it damn well may do," he looked down at his wrist, "in exactly seven minutes."

A headache formed at the base of his skull as Banner pictured the front-page headlines of all three Detroit newspapers if he screwed this one up.

They had been here, twenty-two cops strong, in the middle-class east side Detroit neighborhood for almost three hours. The sun disappeared a half hour ago, but windows stayed open this warm June night of 1943. A soft breeze carried the hint of newly minted elm leaves and somewhere close Kate Smith sang *There'll Be Blue Birds Over the White Cliffs of Dover* on someone's radio.

"Everything under control, Lieutenant?"

Banner turned to a tall, gaunt figure behind him. With the collar of his long trench coat pulled up around his face, Reese Cobb looked like the grim reaper. Cobb, from the Mayor's Office, had a reputation as one of the Police Department's staunchest critics. At the sight of him another knot seemed to twist in the Lieutenant's stomach.

Banner nodded, affecting a coolness he didn't feel. "Hello, Cobb. You just happen to be in the neighborhood?"

"Got a call from one of the taxpayers around here saying there's someone inside holding a woman hostage. The Mayor's always interested when the life of one of his constituents is threatened."

Especially when it's a popular reporter, Banner thought.

"Know who the gunman is?" Cobb had a way of talking without much moving his mouth. In calmer times Banner got a laugh picturing the man with Charley McCarthy setting on his knee. Not tonight.

"Frank Valvano. Small time punk. Works for the mob." Banner reached inside his dark blue uniform jacket for the half-empty pack of Luckies in his shirt pocket. He'd switched to Lucky Strikes when they changed from the old green pack to the new red and white. In a weak moment he'd confess it wasn't taste of the cigarettes that prompted him to change after twenty years of puffing on Chesterfields. He liked the slogan, *Lucky Strike green went to war.* Sounded patriotic.

"He's holding a woman reporter hostage, I hear," Cobb said. "One who works for the *Times*?"

"Name's Kate Brennan." Banner struck a match and held it to his cigarette. If Cobb wanted facts he'd get them, one at a time; pulling them out like wrestling tent stakes from hard ground.

"She the one behind those stories about the mob counterfeiting gasoline rationing coupons?"

Banner shook out the match and dropped it on the ground. He took a deep drag from the Lucky and nodded.

The Mayor's man whistled. "Looks like they're trying to put her out of business." When Banner simply inhaled and blew long trail of smoke into the night air, Cobb spoke again. "Who called you?"

"The woman."

"The woman?"

Banner nodded. "Found Valvano in her living room when she came home. He apparently planned to take her for a ride, one-way. She broke lose, ran into her bedroom and locked the door. She barely had time to phone the switchboard downtown before he forced his way in and grabbed the phone."

"Excuse me, Lieutenant." Wolenski, now out of the squad car, stood next to a man holding a rifle case. "There's a Corporal Harrison here. Says the Chief sent him."

The Corporal stood taller than Banner, well over six feet. He had salt and pepper hair and Banner guessed him to be in his mid-fifties. Banner cocked his head to the side, looking at the man. "The Chief sent . . . who the hell are you?"

"Harrison. Corporal Ben Harrison. Chief thought you might be able to use me." Harrison looked down at his rifle case.

A marksman. The Chief of Police wants him to force the gunman's hand. *What if his marksman misses?* Banner could envision a small trick pony beginning to climb the metal stair to a high board over a water tank in the center ring of a circus somewhere.

"Why haven't I heard your name before, Corporal?"

"Moved up here about a month ago from Nashville, Lieutenant."

"You any good with that thing?" Pointing to the rifle case.

"Get me a clear shot and you'll be home by eleven thirty."

Yeah, if you do my paperwork, Banner thought. But, he took it as a good sign, the guy being confident.

"Where do you want to set up?"

Harrison looked around, then pointed to a thin tree in a front of the house two doors down. "I'll stand over there on the lawn. Use that tree for support."

"The trunk of that tree isn't more than three inches wide. You'll be an easy target."

"Chief said he had a small-caliber pistol. I'll be out of his range. But he won't be out of mine."

"He'll spot you." Banner's nervousness seem to grow by the second. He could see that trick pony on top of the ladder, almost to the diving platform.

"That's the idea. Him knowing there's a rifle pointed at him might cause him to think twice about killing the lady."

"Lieutenant, someone's coming out of the house," Wolenski called.

The gunman, Valvano, had moved onto the porch of the white house, lights from the police cars playing on him like spotlights. He held the woman directly in front of his body, one hand pressing a small pistol tightly to her temple, the other arm wrapped around her upper torso. Only the top half of her face showed, but Banner could see she was an attractive woman, with a thin, straight nose and large, expressive eyes.

"You cops got the car and the grand, or do I kill the woman?"

2

At the sound of the gunman's voice, Harrison began sprinting toward the tree he had spotted two houses down. Ripping the rifle case open as he ran, he checked the clip in the M1 CD. As he reached the tree, he pressed the rifle against its damp trunk.

Through the scope, he could clearly see the pair on the small cement porch. The gunman clutched the woman so close that Harrison couldn't chance a shot. When he saw the man's face just for an instant, it appeared dark and thin with eyebrows that seemed to meet in the middle. Harrison felt shaken by the brutality in the eyes. Some people are born cruel, he thought, cruel and crazy. This woman would die if the guy didn't get what he wanted, no question.

Still looking through the scope, Harrison moved the tip of the rifle muzzle downward. That's when he saw what she was doing and thought, *God, that woman has balls!*

She must have seen him running toward the tree, because she appeared to be signaling to him. She had to be; why else would she be doing that with her fingers? He focused the scope on her hands, held together in front of her. He could see her pointing straight downward with the index finger of her right hand. Then, with her left hand clenched, she extended each of three fingers, one at a time, in a one-two-three counting motion.

God, that woman has balls.

Harrison moved the scope back to the woman's face. She was pretty, and young; and should have been scared out of her wits. Instead of fear, though, her eyes burned with defiance. Screw the bastard with the gun at her head, she seemed to be saying, she was going to hit the ground on the count of three.

But she had to be sure he saw what she was doing.

"Lieutenant!" Harrison fought to get Banner's attention. The Lieutenant was busy calling back and forth to the gunman on the porch, trying to stall, to negotiate. Something. Anything.

"Lieutenant Banner!" Banner finally swung around.

"Lieutenant, have one of your men shine a light on me. I want the two on the porch to see me."

Banner had momentarily forgotten about Harrison, pushing him to the back of his mind, hoping he wasn't serious about shooting at the gunman. No one could be sure of hitting a target that small from way back there. Nearly two hundred feet. And if he missed by just a little . . . Banner could see the pony poised at the end of the diving platform.

But he gave the order and one of the black and white jockeys pointed the spotlight on his car at the rifleman behind the tree. The gunman saw him from the porch, but didn't move, keeping his gun pressed to the woman's temple. Harrison made sure she saw him, holding the M1 sniper rifle against the tree trunk, raising and lowering it slowly three times. Then he called. "Okay, lights out."

Back in the scope, Harrison watched the woman's face and saw by the way her eyes looked straight at him that she had understood. He lowered the scope to look at her hands . . . but they weren't moving. What the hell was she waiting for?

Bringing the scope back up, he saw. The gunman had tightened his grip around the woman's head and neck. No way could she get loose enough to drop. Her lips moved, she said something, maybe asked him to loosen his hold, because that's what he seemed to do as she let out a breath. Her eyes dropped to the ground once again. Harrison lowered his scope to her hands. Again the index finger of her left hand pointed downward. She was ready.

One. Her right index finger shot out.

Two. The middle finger came out and Harrison raised the scope to head level. There would be just one chance.

One shot.

The woman's face now filling his scope, Harrison couldn't see her finger signals. But on what would have been the count of three her head dropped from the frame, exposing Valvano's shocked face for an instant before he moved quickly to raise her up.

Not quickly enough.

The .30-06 slug from the M1, traveling at 2,837 feet per second, tore through the right side of Valvano's scalp, blowing away a portion of his head. His body slammed back against the door of the house, then sagged to a heap on the porch. Having regained her balance the woman stood, hands clenched, glaring down at her would-be-killer lying in a pool of blood rapidly spreading over the porch.

God, that woman has balls.

* * *

You've just met Darcy James' great aunt, Kate Brennan, a 21st Century woman who just happens to live in the 1940s.

The year is 1943 and the Locks at Sault Ste. Marie are the most heavily guarded piece of real estate in North America. Ten thousand U.S. troops are stationed there to guard against a German attack, which could shut down every war materials plant in the United States.

Leaving Detroit and taking a job with her grandfather's newspaper at the Soo, Kate uncovers a secret Nazi plot to blow up the Locks and paralyze the U.S. war effort.

If you liked *Freeze Frame*, you're going to love *Dead Lock*.

Watch for Dead Lock in Autumn of 2007.

Printed in the United States
101062LV00001B/1-48/A